The Second Mount

The Second Mount
Christine Pullein-Thompson

Illustrated

Dragon

Granada Publishing Limited
Published in 1967 by Dragon Books
Frogmore, St Albans, Herts AL2 2NF
Reprinted 1970, 1973, 1976

First published by Burke Publishing Co Ltd 1957
This edition first published by
Atlantic Book Publishing Co Ltd 1967
Copyright © Christine Pullein-Thompson 1957
Made and printed in Great Britain by
C. Nicholls & Company Ltd
The Philips Park Press, Manchester
Set in Intertype Times

The Beginning

"I don't call it a real job. Not a man's job. All right for a girl like Pat with something behind her," Mrs. Smith said.

David looked out of the small cottage window across the neat garden to Church Lane and the elms on the other side. He had always known deep down that his family wouldn't like him going into partnership with Pat; not that she had all the money now, because he had managed to save more than one hundred pounds from the prize money he had won with Folly. But her father was Master of the local hounds; she lived in the Hall, and if she hadn't preferred the idea of running a riding school with David, she would now be being groomed for a debutante season in London.

David had met Pat ages ago when they were both quite young. He had caught her pony when she had fallen off in the hunting field and she had invited him to tea at the Hall. He had found that she was lonely too, living alone with her parents. Later he had become kennel boy at the kennels, in exchange for a pony which had been Sinbad, but which later became Folly, a brown mare which he had jumped successfully at some of the biggest shows in the country.

He remembered all this as he stood in the little cottage kitchen which he knew and loved, while the kettle sang on the old black range, and a pile of washing lay in a chair waiting to be ironed. His mother was rolling out pastry on the plain, scrubbed table. Spring had come, and outside the birds were singing gaily of the summer still to come.

"But, Mum, if I take a job with horses I may never get anywhere. This is my big chance," David said now.

She looked at the cups standing on the mantelpiece. She was tall, dressed in an overall, her grey hair pinned back behind her ears. "I'm only thinking of what's best for

5

you," she said. "Your Dad doesn't mind. He says you're to do what you want, what you've always done; like the others," she added, remembering her other two sons, who had both won scholarships to Cambridge, and Susan, who was now a secretary earning ten pounds a week.

"It's all right, then?" he asked before he went whistling into the garden, down Church Lane, across the Common which held so many memories, to the Hall.

Pat was in the stables grooming her fourteen-two pony, Swallow.

"Hullo. What luck?" she called as David came up the drive.

She had blue eyes and chestnut hair; she was generally laughing, though sometimes she would be overwhelmed by a fit of gloom which would make her silent and depressed. Like David, she was just sixteen. In the autumn she would be leaving school. For years she had planned this riding school with David; from the moment she had heard that the Lane Riding School was giving up she had said, "Why don't we teach? We can start with tots at the week-ends."

David had been against it for a long time; he hadn't felt that they were good enough to teach riding; now, with several years of success in the show jumping world behind him, he felt slightly, but only slightly, more confident.

"It's all right," he said, now joining Pat in the loose box. "But we must make a success of it. I shall never live it down if we don't."

The boys at his school had nicknamed him "The Toff" long ago. Most of them were already in jobs, driving delivery vans, working in shops, on farms, in factories, taking a pound home to their mothers every week. They had laughed at David when he told them he was going into the riding school business. Like his mother, they didn't think he would get anywhere. He hadn't even told Pat some of the things they had said.

"Of course we'll succeed," Pat said. "After all, we've make quite a bit already teaching at week-ends."

6

"But we haven't paid rent; and your father's been paying for Folly's keep."

David was insisting that they paid rent to Colonel Lewisham for the six loose boxes they planned to use, also for the field in front of the house. He didn't want to be indebted or beholden to anyone.

They sat in Swallow's box and started to make plans, and to both of them it was a dream coming true.

"We'll have Mistletoe for the beginners; and Folly and Swallow for the experts. But what about the middle ones?" asked Pat.

"We'll have to buy something," said David.

"We'll need some more tack too," Pat added.

"We'll open on the first day of the summer holidays, don't you think?" asked David.

He was finishing his last term at school; by August he would be free, independent; in front of him seemed to stretch endless opportunities; often he would lie in bed thinking about them, wondering, 'Am I doing the right thing? Am I being fair to Mum?' But, whatever happened, he knew that his life was bound up with horses; nothing could alter that now. He was what his family called "horse mad," and always had been as far back as he could remember.

They went on planning.

"We'll advertise in the 'buses. It isn't very expensive. Advertising is the great thing. If people know we exist, they'll come all right," David said.

"We need a new set of jumps," Pat told him.

"I'll make those between now and the holidays," David said.

"We ought to contact all the local schools. They might like to include riding in their curriculum."

"We should be writing all this down," David said.

"We must mark out a school. We'll need dressage markers. Oh, isn't it all exciting? I never really thought it would happen, did you?" cried Pat.

David's doubts always faded when he was with Pat.

7

"It's marvellous," he cried now. "But we really must make up our minds about a name. We can't even think about the sign until we know what it is called."

"It'll have to have a horse on it. The Hall Riding School sounds so dull, doesn't it?" asked Pat.

"Yes; it does rather," David agreed.

They leaned against the loose box door and thought, while Swallow peacefully chewed hay, and in the distance they could hear the lawn at the Hall being mown for the first time since the winter.

"I can't think of anything. Did your parents really mind?" asked Pat at last.

"Mum did a bit at first," David admitted. "She doesn't think teaching is a man's job."

"But it's only a stepping-stone, isn't it?" Pat asked. "I mean, in the end you mean to jump for England."

"Yes," David replied doubtfully, and that day seemed very far away. He brushed back his dark hair, which was always falling like a forelock across his face so that Susan, who was inclined to be refined, often said, "Oh, David, your hair! Why don't you plaster it with Brylcream or something." He looked across the stable-yard and thought, 'Shall I ever be any good? Shall I ever own a tip-top show jumper of my own? Most of all, shall I ever ride with a Union Jack under my saddle?'

Pat seemed to read his thoughts, for she said, "I'm sure you'll make it. You're one of those people who always does in the end."

"You're such an optimist," replied David.

"Well, I was right last time," she said; and he remembered how determined he had been, when he was ten, to win at all the shows, and how Pat had believed in him and how everything had turned out all right in the end.

It was nearly the end of the holidays. April had come in like a lion, so that everyone had been muddled and thought it was still March. Now she was going out gently with sun and showers and many-coloured rainbows. David dreaded his return to school. Most of his friends had gone on to the

8

Grammar School long ago; he didn't fit in with the remaining boys. He and his brothers had a reputation for getting on in the world, which caused a great deal of spite.

"*Horse and Hound's* in the saddle-room. Shall we look at it?" asked Pat.

The saddle-room smelt of soap and leather; it shone with gleaming bits and stirrups; it was a second home to David. They sat on a chest full of rugs and looked through "Horses for Sale." They marked one or two which might be suitable. They weren't sure what they were looking for.

"Something small and quiet," David said.

"Something of thirteen-two suitable for beginners," argued Pat.

They both knew that they really needed two ponies, but that they couldn't afford it yet, so that they kept hoping one would turn up on loan from somewhere.

They decided which of them would reply to which before they saddled Folly and Swallow and went riding together down familiar lanes, across well-known fields, and home through tall beech woods breaking into leaf.

They continued making plans, and their ponies walked side by side like old friends.

"We really need six ponies altogether. I wonder whether we could get Sinbad back. I know he's awful, but . . ."

"He's not awful!" cried David, who had a soft spot in his heart for Sinbad.

Pat looked at him and thought he looked a little boy again with his forelock dangling over one eye, his laughing face, his voice, which had reverted six years, so that for a moment she had expected to see a small boy of ten again in working boots, jodhs too small, and a jersey knitted by his mother.

David was remembering Sinbad. "He'll teach everyone to stick on. He'll be good for conceited people. He taught me more than anyone," he said.

"I'll speak to Daddy about it. I expect he'll need re-schooling. The Vicar's children aren't much good," Pat said.

"That means four altogether – Folly, Swallow, Mistletoe

9

and Sinbad," calculated David, counting on his fingers.

"But Swallow and Folly aren't much good except for taking people out. At least, they won't be until we've got some good pupils," Pat said.

They had arranged to pay Pat's parents ten pounds a year in rent for the field in front of the house; and thirty pounds a year for the six loose boxes and tack-room. David couldn't help feeling it wasn't enough; but you couldn't argue with Colonel Lewisham, who was small with a large grey moustache and made you think of a ratting terrier, and who was a Master of Foxhounds as well.

They calculated how much oats each pony would consume in a week as they turned for home, and David began to realise that the profit from six ponies would never pay two people's wages. He had a sinking feeling at the pit of his stomach; because, whatever happened, he was determined to pay his mother a pound each week. His brothers had; even John, when he was at Cambridge, had done odd jobs in the vac. so that he wouldn't let his mother down.

"We'll have to deal as well," said David presently, ending what would have been a silence but for the clip-clop of their ponies' hoofs and the birds singing in the hedges.

"It's always a risk. You'll have to do the selling. You know I hate it. I want to keep everything," Pat replied.

He knew she loathed parting with any horse. She had often cried when the Hunt had sold one in the past – a horse she had hardly known at all.

"We'll have to harden our hearts," said David, looking at her nose, which turned up at the end.

They came to the stable-yard, to dogs dreaming in the sun, to Hunt horses looking over loose box doors, to doves cooing, and the clank of buckets. They put their ponies away and stood talking together till David turned for home with the two advertisements he was to answer in his pocket.

They were just beginning tea when David reached the cottage. Susan was there, tall in high heels.

"You been with Pat again? People will start talking," she said.

"Why should they? We're not the first people to go into business together," he replied, thinking how lovely it would be to see a string of ponies crossing the Common again, as they had when he was ten. 'And they'll be ours,' he thought, and for a moment he was filled with hope and ambition which defeated the doubts still lurking in his mind. In front of him stretched the years brimming with success, until on one glorious day he stood in a foreign stadium in scarlet coat acknowledging the cheers of the crowd, knowing that he had jumped successfully for England.

Mrs. Smith ended his dream. "Don't stand there. Sit down and have some tea while it's still hot," she said.

Suzy

So gradually their dream came true: David made jumps; Sinbad, ugly, black and bad-tempered, came back to the Hall; they called their stable the Elm Tree Riding School, named after the tree which stood at the end of the drive. The gardens were yellow with daffodils. Swallow and Folly were turned out to rest after the hunting season. Pat started to ride her first pony, Mistletoe, for half an hour each evening. And all the time David was wondering, 'Shall we ever make enough? Am I doing the right thing? Is it really wrong for me to be running a riding school with Pat?'

Now he had made up his mind, his mother was behind him, as though she had always wanted him to have a career with horses. Susan had stopped talking about it; but the boys at school went on chaffing him, and often he would think 'Perhaps they're right after all.'

June came scorching without a breath of air, or so it seemed to David. They still hadn't bought a pony. They had gone by train, 'bus and bicycle to look at three, but either they were more than they could afford or unsuitable.

11

But it was only June and there was still July before they opened officially on the first of August.

Presently the local and Oxford 'buses were splashed with their advertisement: *Riding? The Elm Tree Riding School is opening on August 1st. Excellent Hacking. Lessons. First-class Horses and Ponies* was how it ran, and their address and telephone number were at the bottom. Colonel Lewisham had had a telephone put in the saddle-room for them.

"Otherwise the 'phone will be ringing all day in the house, driving us mad," he said.

Only one thing worried them about their advertisement, and that was the word "horses," because, as Pat said, they hadn't any horses yet; and, of course, that was true, because Folly and Swallow were both under fourteen-two.

But they both meant to get something larger as soon as possible, and in the meantime they didn't want to put off grown-ups by mentioning only the word "ponies."

They were both working hard at the week-ends in preparation for A Test, which they intended to take in the summer. They spent some of David's hundred pounds having a brochure printed and on writing paper with their address at the top. It was all tremendously exciting, and often David couldn't sleep at night, but lay tossing and turning, doing accounts in his head, trying to forget what the boys at his school said, remembering that his life was his own to do what he liked with.

July came and they found a pony. She was advertised in the local paper: *Skewbald mare, thirteen hands, quiet to ride and in traffic.* David's father took them to see her in the van, which smelt of fish.

They fell in love with her at once. She had a kind eye and a well-tapered muzzle. She was attractively marked, short in the leg, with neat, two-coloured hoofs.

She belonged to a farmer who had bought her for his daughter. "But Betty never took to riding and I hate to see the pony standing there doing nothing," he said.

David's father stayed in the background. David and Pat

12

tried to appear older than they were. They felt the mare's legs in a professional manner, looked at her teeth and eyes, turned her this way and that.

"What do you call her?" Pat asked, and the farmer said "Suzy."

"I like her, don't you?" Pat whispered to David. They each rode Suzy in turn. She had good head carriage, but her stride was on the short side, and each time they passed the gate she tried to stick.

"She's a good pony. I bought her from a dealer. He got her off some gipsies," the farmer said.

"I expect she goes in harness, then," remarked Pat. They had each ridden Suzy now and they stood looking at her, trying to make up their minds.

"How much do you want for her?" asked Pat at last.

She was eight years old and he wanted forty pounds for her. David said "Won't you take less?" without much hope.

Pat stood back and looked at her again while David thought 'We've done everything wrong. We should have pulled her to pieces. Instead, we've admired her kind eye, and said she looks exactly what we're looking for.'

"Well, what do you think?" muttered Pat, taking him on one side. "I like her a lot. I think yes."

'It'll leave us with a little under sixty pounds,' thought David. "I wish he would take less," he said; but he won't though, he thought at the same time.

In the end they paid forty pounds for Suzy and took it in turns to ride her home through the warm July evening.

"I don't think we could have done better. She's really awfully sweet," Pat said.

"Only another week and then we open," David said, and his mouth felt dry at the thought.

They had had several enquiries. Two or three people had already booked up for Bank Holiday week-end. They had decided to give the local show a miss, partly because there were no classes suitable for Swallow and Folly, but mostly because they wanted to take as many pupils as possible without overworking the ponies during the first few weeks.

13

"I know; and there still seems so much to do," said Pat. They turned out Suzy with the other ponies and stood watching while she rolled.

"I wonder how she's bred," said David; and Pat said, "New Forest, I should think."

Pat fetched sandwiches and a plate of rock cakes and mugs of steaming tea from the Hall, and they sat in the saddle-room and talked about Suzy and how pretty she was, and how one always had to pay more for skewbald ponies, until they had convinced themselves that Suzy was a bargain for forty pounds.

"And, anyway, if she doesn't turn out to be just what we want, we can school her a bit and sell her for fifty," said David.

"I don't think we'll want to do that," replied Pat quickly. "She's so sweet, and children always love a skewbald."

It was Saturday, and when David reached home his father had gone to the pub, and Michael, his married brother, was sitting on the kitchen table swinging his legs.

"How goes it? How's the business?" he asked. And David, who had become shy about the riding school, only said, "All right, thank you." And his mother came in with a pile of washing and said, "You bought the pony, then?"

David was thinking: 'Supposing she's a dud? We ought to have got a vet to look at her.' He said, "Yes, That's right," and imagined Suzy standing on her hind legs and then falling slowly over backwards. We won't even be able to give her a warranty then, he thought, and for a moment he was filled with an awful sense of foreboding, and for the first time he wished that he had taken a safe job with a weekly wage packet at the end.

But next morning the sense of foreboding had vanished as he walked down to Elm Tree Riding School while the church bells called Christians to Communion, and the Common was swathed in the peace of Sunday, and only one car and an old man on a bicycle meandered down Church Lane.

They had decided to ride all the ponies; it was the last week-end before the end of term.

As David strolled into the yard with the sun behind him, it seemed the sort of day when nothing could go wrong. Pat wasn't there, and David hesitated before he took two halters from a hook in the saddle-room and crossed the yard and opened a gate and was in the field which ran in front of the Hall.

"Co'up, co'up," he called, and there was dew on the grass and on the dazzling buttercups and daisies. All his fears of yesterday seemed silly now. The future seemd blessed like the morning. Nothing could go wrong. He whistled as he walked towards the ponies grazing. He thought: 'Only one more week and after that freedom.' Folly turned and whinnied when she saw him; the other ponies raised their heads. Suzy stood alone. 'They're treating her like a new girl,' David thought, and then he saw her move and his heart stood still. He saw now that her whole near foreleg was swollen and there were streaks of blood on her forearm and cannon bone, and all the beauty seemed to leave the morning and he was alone with disaster, standing amid the buttercups and daisies.

He thought: 'What will Pat say? Only one more week. Why did it have to happen now?' before he approached Suzy, whispering soft words, saying "Poor old Suzy," over and over again, while his mind was one leap ahead, imagining pupils with nothing to ride, a dwindling bank balance, the people who would say, "We told you so."

She was friendly and pathetic with her large, kind eyes and the leg that she didn't like to put to the ground. He knelt in the grass and looked at the cut, which had stopped bleeding and lay slantwise across her forearm, and she blew down his neck and nuzzled his shoulder, and he said again, "Poor old Suzy," and "Did one of them kick you?"

He stood up and slipped a halter over her small chestnut ears, and shouted at the other ponies when they approached, because Suzy had started to move and to tremble.

15

Then he saw Pat coming towards him, and she cried, "What's happened? What's wrong with Suzy?"

He pointed to her foreleg and called back, "Kicked." She shouted, "What?"

And he yelled "Kicked" again and she started to run.

The other ponies had started to graze again, and the church bells were ringing, so the early service was over. Pat hadn't combed her hair, and her eyes were still clouded with sleep.

"Oh dear, why did it have to happen?" she cried, stopping beside David, looking at the leg, thinking: 'She'll be lame for ages; it'll mean buying another pony.'

"We'll have to get the vet," David said. "She can hardly walk. It's lucky it didn't sever the artery," and he imagined Suzy bleeding to death alone in the moonlight all through the long night.

Pat said a word she wasn't allowed to use. "Oh, why did it have to happen?" she asked again.

David was saying "Come on, Suzy," and leading her gently across the field. The church bells had stopped ringing, and now there was nothing to tell you that it was Sunday, and the future looked tired and without hope, and David thought, 'I wonder how much the vet will charge?'

'It is unfair,' Pat thought. 'Why does it have to happen to us? Ponies *are* beastly sometimes. What will the vet say? Supposing she's lame the whole summer?'

They put Suzy into one of the loose boxes before they went to the saddle-room and telephoned.

"I wish it wasn't Sunday. I always think it's cheek telephoning a vet on a Sunday," Pat said.

"I expect it's all in the day's work. After all, we're going to work on Sundays," David replied.

"But we shall rest on Mondays," pointed out Pat.

The vet said that he would be over soon after ten, so after they had bathed Suzy's leg they caught the other ponies and groomed them.

"And now we'll have to hang about and wait," said Pat, putting a dandy brush back into the saddle-room.

"Oh, why did it have to happen?" she asked

The vet was tall, dressed in twill trousers, a checked shirt and hacking jacket.

"I didn't know you existed. I didn't know there was a riding school in these parts," he said.

"Well, we aren't existing yet; not till next week," Pat explained.

He looked at Suzy's leg, felt her forearm, said, "Did someone kick you, my dear?"

Folly started to kick her door because she was jealous; Sinbad tried to bite Mistletoe.

"She's badly bruised. It's a clean cut. The swelling should go down in a few days; if it doesn't, give it a go with the hose-pipe twice a day. I'll give you some powder for the cut," the vet said, straightening his back.

"Should we keep her in?" asked David.

"How long will she be lame?" asked Pat.

"No. She'll be better walking about, but put her by herself. She'll probably be lame for three or four weeks," the vet replied.

David thought: For most of the holidays. Pat said, "Oh dear. We only bought her yesterday."

"Hard luck," said the vet, fetching a carton of powder from the car. "Put this on twice a day and keep it clean. I'm just going to give her an anti-tet. injection," he said, handing Pat the carton, saying "Steady, my dear," as he slid the needle into Suzy's neck.

"There we are, then. Ring me up if it looks nasty or anything," he said, shutting the boot of his car, before he drove away through the bright July morning.

Pat and David stood feeling flat.

"I suppose we might as well ride," said Pat at last. Neither of them felt like it. They felt that Fate was against their business and David couldn't help thinking: 'Supposing another one goes lame?'

"We'd better turn her out in the paddock behind the kennels. Daddy won't mind," said Pat.

They led Suzy down the lane to the kennels, which smelt

18

of flesh and hound and old bones. There was plenty of grass in the paddock.

"She'll probably have laminitis next," said David.

"Oh, don't be so defeatist!" cried Pat, slamming the paddock gate. "Things are bound to go wrong sometimes."

"I suppose we'll have to buy another horse or pony or something," said David, thinking of his hundred pounds, which had become fifty-five, and was soon to shrivel even more.

'It's not that I'm stingy,' he thought. 'It's just that I like to have something in hand for what Mum calls a "rainy day".' He remembered his father saying once, "Never owe money, son. Never spend what you haven't got." And the evils of hire purchase was one of his mother's favourite subjects.

"There's not much time. That's the trouble," Pat said.

"There's the horse sale on Friday. We could try there," David said, remembering that once they had agreed never to buy at a sale.

"It's rather a risk," replied Pat.

"We could buy something warranted. Time's running out, you know," David answered. He felt angry with Pat, angry with everything. The whole day was ruined now. Nothing was left of the mood which had carried him so blissfully to the stables only a couple of hours ago.

"I haven't had any breakfast yet," said Pat, walking on ahead down the lane, thinking it's too nice a morning to be cross. Accidents are bound to happen; it's no good being disagreeable about them.

When Pat had had breakfast, they both felt better. They agreed that they would go to the sale with an open mind, and that they wouldn't buy anything unless it was absolutely what they wanted and had a warranty as well. And then they schooled and jumped the ponies, and booked up two more pupils who telephoned.

David didn't tell his family about Suzy, partly because he didn't want to depress his mother and partly because he was afraid Susan would keep asking questions and wondering how long his hundred pounds would last.

After lunch he and Pat put up the jumps David had made, and they had tea together and wandered down to the kennels and bathed Suzy's leg again.

When David fell asleep that night, he dreamed of the sale, and that Suzy was there standing in a pen with blood dripping from her foreleg.

The Horse Sale

The sale began at eleven o'clock. It was held monthly in the market of a neighbouring town. Pat and David arrived there soon after nine o'clock dressed in riding clothes, full of resolutions, anxious not to buy rather than to buy.

Early in the morning it had drizzled; now the sun was shining from a chequered sky.

"Daddy says we're idiotic coming here and that we're *not* to buy," said Pat for the second time.

"Dad says the same," remarked David.

All the same they were both filled with a pleasant sense of adventure and imagined themselves leading a future prize-winner home through the summer evening.

They had come in by 'bus. David's mother had given him a packet of sandwiches, a slice of cake, apples, a flask of tea – enough for both of them, it turned out.

The market was full of cracking whips, men in gaiters, children prodding calves with sticks, horses standing tied in the long hall where later they would be sold.

Pat and David went up and down these horses, and all the time more kept coming in. They felt their legs and looked at their eyes and teeth, and there seemed at least six they wanted to buy.

"But we mustn't," David said.

They bought a catalogue, and cups of tea at a buffet.

The whole place smelt of animals – of cows and pigs,

sheep and horses. They went back to the long hall bedded with peat. The auctioneer had arrived, and someone called Charlie, who held a long whip, the longest David had ever seen. One horse was neighing pitifully, another was wind-sucking, a third dug up the peat with his hoofs.

"We must be business-like. We ought to mark our cata-logue," David said.

Most of the horses had arrived by now. Old and young, large and small, hack and hunter, vanner, pony, cart-horse, cob – there was a huge variety; every conceivable colour was there, every kind of fault in conformation – sickle-hocks, cow-hocks, goose-rumps; herring-gutted, narrow-chested, broad-chested, ewe-necked, high-crested, flatsided, long-backed, hollow-backed, even roach-backed horses were there. And there were some horses so lovely that David wondered why they were there among the scum, the misunderstood, the neglected, the maltreated of the horse world.

Pat wanted to buy one old cart pony which had sores where the collar had rubbed. David fell in love with a dark bay mare, with a head which pulled at your heart-strings, long, sloping shoulders, short cannon bones and a hint of a goose-rump.

"If only we were millionaires," sighed Pat.

"We could buy them all then," said David, looking round the hall, longing for a million pounds to drop into his hand.

"Well, if the old pony goes for less than ten, let's buy her, and if this bay goes for under forty-five let's buy her," suggested David.

"But neither of them will be any good in the school," cried Pat, thinking: 'He's gone mad. He's worse than I am.'

"I mean as specs," replied David, who had picked up the word from his brother John. "We might sell the old mare for twelve pounds when she's had a holiday to a good home, and the bay mare we can re-school and sell at a handsome profit."

"If she's re-schoolable," said Pat.

They found a small, brown Dartmoor warranted sound

and quiet in traffic and they wrote "Thirty" beside her. They looked at a useful, short-backed cob suitable for adults or teenage children and they wrote "Forty" beside him. Then they waited for the sale to begin.

And we vowed we wouldn't buy anything, remembered David, and his legs felt weak and his tummy was suddenly empty, and he said, "Here, let's eat my sandwiches."

Pat was thinking: 'What will Daddy say if we take a horse home?'

She took a sandwich, said "Thank you" with a mind still far away at the Hall, facing her father, saying, "She was only ten pounds" or "She's a spec" or "He'll be very useful in the riding school." And there'll be Austin, the Hunt stud groom, to face, she remembered, and she thought 'But why does it matter what they think?' And knew that it did matter, because she didn't want to hurt them, nor to hurt herself, nor to have helped spend David's money on a failure.

The auctioneer was on his stand now, with a clerk sitting directly below. A little sun filtered through the skylights in the roof. The hall was stiflingly hot and stank of horse. Pat said "I think I'm going to faint" in a whisper and put her head between her knees.

David grabbed her shoulders; but she didn't faint, and she came up a moment later saying, "I'm sorry. I felt just as though I was passing out."

Her chestnut hair had fallen across her face, which was quite colourless.

"You'd better come out for a second. It's stifling in here," David said.

"But we'll miss everything," protested Pat.

"No; we won't. It's the cart-horses first," David replied.

They stood outside for a time, and Pat said, "I'm sorry to be such a drip," and David said, "It doesn't matter."

When they returned to the hall Charlie was chasing a black Shire with his whip, while a tiny man ran at the horse's head, and the auctioneer was calling, "I'm bid fifty, fifty, fifty, fifty – thank you, sir – fifty-one. . . ." And the air was full of the smell of churned peat and sweating horses, and the sun beat on the iron roof; and now that the horse was standing still, sweating and trembling, people dragged his mouth open, felt his legs, slapped his rump. Pat wanted to take the whip from Charlie and drive away the people who were mauling the Shire; she wanted to take him home and turn him out in green fields. But the hammer fell. "Fifty-five, to you, sir," called the auctioneer. And a tall woman in riding clothes turned to her daughter and said, "Meat. What a shame!"

Pat and David didn't look at one another, but they knew that they were filled with the same sadness. There was nothing to say because of that.

A bay vanner was led up next with more whip-cracking, and David wondered why they had ever looked forward to coming; they were pushed and crushed while they tried to watch, and once a tall farmer, thickset and burly, stood on Pat's foot until in desperation she said, "Please can you move?"

But at last the little black pony was run up; in spite of the crowd, her eyes remained dull, as though nothing would ever surprise her again. She was warranted quiet to drive and sound, but all the same the bidding didn't start until Pat nudged David, who called out "Seven" in a clear voice. After that an old man nodded his head and bid nine and the man who had bought the Shire raised his hand and the auctioneer called, "Ten. I'm bid ten."

"Bid again. Bid eleven," Pat hissed and David bid eleven; eventually she went for thirteen to the man who had bought the Shire and two large tears stood in Pat's eyes and David said, "Perhaps it's the best thing after all. She'll probably have a rest first," and he thought of the little pony meeting her fate, and if he had been ten he would have felt like crying too.

They went outside and bought cups of tea and returned to watch the riding horses sold.

"I can't help thinking we should have bid fourteen," Pat said.

"And then the meat man would have bid fifteen," David replied.

They stopped and watched a hunter sold for a hundred guineas which was fully warranted and had been hunted for three seasons and was evidently known to people. They saw a dun pony sold for forty guineas, and a piebald for forty-five.

"Some of them fetch quite good prices after all," said Pat, surprised.

They saw the cob they had marked on their catalogue sold for forty-seven, and a Shetland pony for twenty-five. Then the bay mare came up, and for a time no one bid, though the auctioneer called, "Come along, ladies and gentlemen. Here's a nice mare, a very nice mare. Here's blood if you like. Who's going to bid? Fifty, forty ... come along now."

No one stepped forward to look at the bay. David consulted his catalogue. He read: *Bay Mare. Eight years old. Warranted sound.* So it's her manners which are wrong, he thought.

Pat was biting her nails with impatience. 'Isn't anyone going to bid,' she thought. 'What does she do? Where is the meat man?' She glanced round and saw that he had gone, and supposed that he had bought his quota for the day. 'Daddy will be furious if we buy her,' she thought. All the same, she turned to David and said, "Aren't you going to bid?"

But at that moment a man in jodhpurs murmured, "Twenty," and the auctioneer shouted, "Twenty. I'm bid twenty. Come along now. This mare is worth more than twenty."

The bidding went slowly up. Twice David bid, though he kept thinking: 'We don't really want her. What could we do with her? She's probably impossible.' Finally, he said, "Forty," and thought with relief: 'Now I needn't bid any more. Someone else will bid and we won't be saddled with her.' He waited, and then his heart started to thump because there was no immediate bid. The auctioneer went on calling,

24

"Forty. I'm bid forty." And David thought: 'What have I done?' before the hammer fell and, turning to David, the auctioneer said, "Name, please?"

"D. Smith," he answered while he thought again: 'What have I done?'

The clerk wrote down his name while the mare was led away and tied up again.

"Well, she's ours now," said Pat in a flat voice.

"Yes; for better or worse," David replied.

"Daddy will be furious," remarked Pat. "We've done just what he warned us not to do."

"Well, it's done now."

They went across and looked at the mare, and suddenly, as she stood resting a hind leg, she was ugly. Her neck looked thin, her goose-rump bony; her ears were too large, David thought.

'What did we see in her before?' wondered Pat.

'Gosh! I feel a fool,' thought David.

'What will Mr. Austin say,' mused Pat. "We'll have to think of a name," she said.

"If she's too awful I suppose we can send her back here next month," David said.

"And drop ten pounds."

"Not if the meat man's here."

"You are awful," said Pat.

They patted the bay mare, and David said, "We ought to have brought a halter."

"We might as well take her in the one she's wearing. It's probably all in the forty guineas," replied Pat.

David went away and paid two fat men sitting in an office for the bay mare. The whole market filled him with distaste now.

'What fools we've been,' he thought, walking back to find Pat.

They meant to walk and ride the bay mare home. But when David legged up Pat, she bucked her straight off on

She bucked her straight off

to the hard tarmac road outside the market. Several women rushed forward and an elderly man called, "Are you all right, missy?"

Someone said, "What a shame. On that hard tarmac too."

Pat sat on the pavement rocking herself backwards and forwards, holding her head and moaning, "I'm all right, thank you."

The bay mare continued to buck while David clung desperately to the halter rope. A crowd assembled. People dragged their children away and stood at a distance watching the rodeo display.

"She's never been broken. Eight years old and unbroken. Her father was a killer too," said a man in a hacking jacket.

She came to a standstill at last and stood trembling. "She's insane," David thought. His hands were sawed by the rope. He had no breath left.

From somewhere a doctor had appeared and Pat was on her feet now, saying "I'm quite all right, thank you. There's nothing wrong. I'm all right" in decisive tones, while an interfering woman said, "Came a proper smack she did; right on her 'ead too."

'This won't do our reputation any good,' thought David, hating the bay mare for hurting Pat, wishing that they'd never seen her and thinking that it would be tea-time when they reached home.

"Are you all right?" he called to Pat.

"Yes. Fine," she replied, and thanked the doctor and came across and said, "Let's go home. I'm sick of today. I wish it was over."

She had a lump as big as an egg on the back of her head and a stiff neck.

"I should have ridden her. But I didn't expect her to do anything while she was being led. And I wanted you to have first ride," David said.

"It would have been just as bad if you had fallen off," replied Pat.

It was a dismal walk home and nothing happened to dispel

27

their gloom. The sun continued shining. The bay mare was nervous; whenever she saw a gutter, a piece of paper or a stationary car she stuck, and it would be several minutes before she'd walk on again.

"What shall we call her?" asked Pat once.

"Maniac," replied David.

"Don't be silly," said Pat crossly.

'Everything is against us,' thought David. 'First Suzy is kicked, then this happens; and both of them are entirely our fault, because we needn't have put Suzy with the other horses nor bid for this mare. It's we who are maniacs.'

"We should give her a nice name; then she might become nice," Pat said.

"What an idea!" replied David.

They were both cross, and because of that wanted to hurt one another, and they were still a long way from home.

"You're just in a bad temper," Pat said.

"Well, what about you?"

"I've got a headache," Pat replied.

"I'm sorry, then," David said. "Shall we stop somewhere and get some aspirins?"

"No, thank you," replied Pat, wondering why they had ever thought of running a riding school together.

She wants to sulk, thought David.

They walked on and on, while the day grew hotter, and in the fields the last of the hay was being carried, and the wheat and oats and barley stood green and gold. Far away they could see jet planes glinting in the sun, and sometimes an American truck would pass full of Service-men. There were tourists already in one of the little grey villages they walked through, and white ducks swimming on a pond and a smell of flowers blown from the gardens.

The bay mare was walking more easily now and David noticed that her stride was long, though her pasterns were a little short for perfection.

They came at last to the stables, and to their surprise there was no one there and they felt relieved.

"We'd better keep her in for tonight, hadn't we?" Pat

asked. "We don't want her kicked too."

They put her in a box and she stood wide-eyed staring over the door.

"We might call her Wanderer, because she looks like one," suggested David.

"It's too long," replied Pat.

"I might as well go home," said David.

"I'll keep an eye on her," replied Pat.

He walked home soberly and remembered that tomorrow was Saturday, their opening day, and that they had two pupils at ten o'clock.

His mother was putting out the tea things.

"You're early. Did you get anything?" she asked.

"Yes; but she isn't any good," David said, feeling weary beyond words.

His mother said, "I'm just going to make some tea. What's the matter with her?"

David sank down in the comfortable chair which always stood on the left of the range, winter and summer.

"We shouldn't have bought her," he began, and remembered how near he had come to quarrelling with Pat and how she had nearly fainted in the hall, how the tears had come to her eyes when the black pony was sold for meat.

The First Days

Saturday was fine – fine and warm and sunlit without a cloud in the sky.

David, awaking, glancing out of the window of his bedroom, rubbing his eyes, thought: 'Why have I this feeling of calamity?' Then he remembered the bay mare, and the day he had looked forward to for so long became a day to be dreaded. What will we do with her? What will Colonel Lewisham say? he wondered, climbing out of bed, dressing without enthusiasm.

It was early. The kitchen appeared forlorn without his mother. He had made the tea when she came down the stairs in felt slippers, sleepy-eyed, older in the morning light.

"You're not going out without breakfast," she said firmly, fetching bread from the bin, poking the fire, while David poured the tea.

As he ate his breakfast he thought sarcastically: *'Another day of opportunities. Misused ones, lost ones,'* he added to himself.

His mother gave him a bundle of sandwiches and cake for his lunch, and he was ashamed because she was so good and he was cross.

The church clock was striking eight as he hurried across the Common trying to change his mind, thinking: 'I mustn't quarrel with Pat.'

The bay mare was staring over her loose box door and for a moment his heart stood still because she looked so lovely. Her head pulled at his heart strings as it had in the market. Her coat glistened like polished mahogany. He couldn't defeat a feeling of pride as he looked at her. And she's ours, he thought, before he recalled how she had bucked off Pat, how she had stuck and shied all the way home. *Handsome is as handsome does*, he thought. We would have done better to buy something ugly, something reliable which would have earned its keep.

He filled up the bay mare's hay-net and fetched fresh water. She was nervous in the box and dodged him whenever he went in. He wondered what her past had been. Had her sire really been a killer? Had she never been broken? Or had people tried and failed?

Pat came into the yard riding her dark brown Swallow, which so nearly matched Folly, leading little grey Mistletoe, black Sinbad, while Folly dawdled behind.

She waved. "Have you thought of a name?" she asked.

"No. I forgot all about it."

"I thought of Hurricane, Tornado, Whirlpool, Avalanche," Pat said, dismounting, handing him the end of Sinbad's halter. "She needs a fiery name."

"Tornado's the best. To be quite honest, I don't really care," he said.

"Well, it's no good being gloomy about her. She's ours for the time being."

"What did your father say?" he asked.

"Lots of things, some of them unrepeatable, mostly that we needn't think he's going to pull us out of the fire. Not that he means a word of it," said Pat with a laugh. "Mummy wasn't too pleased, either. They both think we're crazy."

"I think they're just about right," said David.

"Well, I think we're going to prove we're not. Where's your spirit? We'll make a success of Tornado, even if she kills us in the process," Pat replied with conviction.

But at that moment David didn't think they would. The future looked black indeed. He had started to think, 'How am I going to take a pound home each week? In three weeks we'll be bankrupt.'

"I've worked out a plan," announced Pat, handing her desolate partner a dandy brush. "Every day we'll put a saddle on Tornado, at first without stirrups, then with them, then with stirrups dangling, then with sacks of straw dangling on each side; then we'll take her for walks with the sacks, lunge her. . . . Do you get the idea?"

"Yes; it sounds pretty good," said David.

Pat took out two girls for an hour's ride at ten o'clock. They rode Sinbad and Mistletoe; she escorted them on Swallow.

In the meantime, David talked to Tornado, patted her trembling neck, felt her legs, but failed to calm her enough to be able to slip a saddle on her arched back.

There were no more pupils till the afternoon, when he would be taking a girl of six on the leading rein. That means a day's takings of twenty-one shillings, he thought, leaving Tornado, beginning to tidy up the boxes before the others' return.

That first day passed without incident. They finished with further bookings in their diary, with a feeling of accomplishment, with more hope in the future than David had felt for some time.

Suzy was better; her swelling was down, and, though she still limped, she walked boldly now, and came across the field to greet Pat and David when they went to treat her in the evening.

"Perhaps she won't be so long after all," said Pat.

They had two classes the next morning, and an adult in the afternoon who rode Folly. They took thirty-seven and six, and David began to feel more certain of the pound he meant to give his mother.

Tornado was quieter. She no longer cringed when they entered the box, and on this day they managed to slip a saddle on her back and girth it up while she stood trembling.

'Who knows, we may make something of her after all' thought David, admiring her head again, wondering if she would jump, what her gallop would be like.

"She should jump with that goose-rump," remarked Pat, seeming to read his thoughts.

"She should. But will she?" David said.

"We must try to find out more about her," Pat told David as they stood later together in the saddle-room beneath the modest array of rosettes which they had won between them during the last five years.

"I don't know how," David said.

"We'll have to make a plan. Spend a day at the market chatting to people," suggested Pat.

They left it at that. They were very busy during the next few days. The telephone was always ringing; they could not fit in all the people as often as they wanted to come. They took classes of children in the field. They gave jumping lessons. They started to lead Tornado along the lanes, two sacks of straw swinging from her saddle. Her confidence was growing. When she whinnied to them one morning, they felt like cheering.

"She must be beginning to like us," Pat cried.

"Or be very hungry," replied David, laughing.

By now he had ceased to worry. They managed to pay themselves each thirty shillings a week, though how they would fare when the horses needed hay they didn't yet know.

Even Susan had stopped making remarks about their partnership, and Mrs. Smith was inclined to boast about David, which embarrassed him.

She would say, "David's doing very well for himself. He's teaching riding – making quite a success of it, too."

He would say, "Touch wood," and turn away from his mother to look out of the window if he was in the cottage, or gaze at the landscape if he was outside.

His father would only say occasionally, "How are you doing, son?"

Presently Suzy was sound again, and though she wasn't as reliable as Mistletoe, she was popular with the more experienced pupils. Sinbad was behaving better than they had expected, and Swallow and Folly were getting quite a lot of work.

Pat's parents looked at Tornado, and though they shook their heads when she snorted at them and retreated to the back of her box, they had to admit that she was good-looking, and if she was ever rideable possessed considerable prospects.

"But I doubt that she will be," said Colonel Lewisham gravely.

"Do be careful. Don't ride her too soon, and remember to wear hard hats," said Mrs. Lewisham, making Pat feel a child again.

And so everything seemed successful: the days were long and fine; their school prospered; Tornado became calm; they received a letter from the Headmistress of St. Helen's School for Girls which seemed to cap the feeling of success that hung over everything.

33

The Headmistress wrote a very agreeable letter. She wanted to know their terminal fees, how many girls they could take, whether they gave jumping tuition.

When they had finished reading the letter, Pat cried, "Isn't it wonderful? Now we'll be all right. We'll have a steady income in term time. Oh, aren't we lucky?"

"How much shall we charge?" asked David.

They made plans. They worked out days and hours and ponies, and wrote to the Headmistress by return of post. They decided to charge three guineas per pupil per term.

"It'll even out over the year," said Pat. "Because in the summer term they'll have much more than three guineas' worth of riding."

David told his mother.

"You *are* getting on," she said.

"Well done, son," his father said.

"We must try to get another pony before then. Something about fourteen hands, don't you think?" asked Pat.

"How old will they be? They don't take big girls, do they?" said David, suddenly thinking: 'Supposing they're older than us? Supposing they refuse to do what we tell them? Or know more than us?'

"Oh, I think they take them right up to school-leaving age and even older," Pat replied.

"How complicated. They may know more than us," said David, who was generally shy with girls of his own age, never felt he got on with them, and was often tongue-tied in their presence.

"But we needn't teach them all. We can take the older ones for hacks," Pat replied.

"You can. I think I shall stay behind and clean tack," David said.

"You are a goat," replied Pat, laughing.

They couldn't believe anything could go wrong now. Fate seemed with them. They slept soundly, wakened early, and in front of them seemed to stretch a long succession of happy days. Then suddenly without warning everything was black again; tragedy came with a mellow September

34

day when the orchards were full of apples, the corn was being carried, and they had backed Tornado for the first time.

The Runaway

It happened on a hot September day, so hot that there seemed hardly a breath of air anywhere; the sort of day which makes you quarrel with your best friend.

Pat and David had altered the afternoon class till the evening; but it was still hot when they saddled the ponies. Everything wilted; there were flies everywhere. The sky was a clear, relentless blue. It seemed that a heat wave had arrived with September; people were talking about an Indian summer still to come.

Pat was telling David about the evening class. He had only taken out one of the children before. It was two days since they had written to the Headmistress of St. Helen's; they were expecting a reply at any time. They were still very optimistic as they stood in the yard talking, while near them were their six horses and ponies, clean and shining, their tails like spun silk.

"Peter's not very good. I let him off the lead for the first time last time; but he should be all right on Mistletoe," Pat said. "Judy's rather nervous, but quite firm as long as she doesn't panic. She's inclined to scream, though." She was to ride Sinbad.

"John's jumped at home. His seat's awful. If anything goes wrong, he tips forward and clutches the pony's neck. He's not at all nervous, though," continued Pat. He was to ride Suzy. Lastly, there was Julia, a tall, pale girl who had a 'pash' on David. She was fifteen and had ridden in London as a child occasionally. Now she seemed to have outgrown her strength. She was to ride Swallow.

"I shall go somewhere quiet, through the beech woods and back across the Common," said David.

"Let's hope none of them want to canter. If only Tornado was sensible, I could have come too," said Pat.

Presently the pupils came; first Judy, small and pretty, with fair curly hair and the face of an elf.

"Am I riding Mistletoe? Oh, hurray," she cried. Pat helped her up.

"I am going off the lead, aren't I?" she asked.

"Yes. That's right," Pat said.

It seemed to be growing hotter every moment. Nothing stirred the trees. It's thundery, David thought, as John came up the drive wheeling his bicycle.

"Hullo," he called. "I'm not late, am I?"

He was strong and fair, with blue eyes, and looked good at games.

"No. Early," David shouted.

When he heard he was to ride Suzy, he said, "How wizard." He hadn't ridden her before. He put himself up; David only checked his stirrups.

Peter had a small, peaky face. He wore a brown crash cap with elastic under his chin. He and Julia came up the drive together. She had her hair tied back with a ribbon. She smiled at David.

When they were all up, David mounted Folly and led the way down the drive.

"We're going through Stony Bottom Woods and back across the Common. I hope that's all right for everybody," he said.

"I went that way last time," grumbled Judy.

"Wizard," exclaimed John.

"The woods will be nice and cool," remarked Julia.

Peter was humming to himself. He never bothered to talk much to the other children; he lived in his own private world, and when you spoke to him he always said, "What?" which gave him time to collect his wits before he replied.

David was big for his brown Folly now, too big to hunt her for a whole day any more, too big to jump her much. His feet were well below her elbows, but in spite of this she carried him easily and it was David, not her, who worried about his weight.

He kept looking back to watch his class, and every time Julia would catch his eye and smile so that he found himself avoiding her face, looking over her head if he could. The ponies seemed quiet enough. He corrected John's seat, told Peter to shorten his reins a little, Julia to sit further forward in the saddle, Judy to keep her hands down. After that he relaxed a little.

Presently they came to the woods, rode under trees which met in arches above their heads, until they were in the heart of the woods, which were still, but cool after the glaring heat outside.

"Aren't they lovely?" exclaimed Julia.

"Wizard!" agreed John.

David said, "I'm trotting on," pushed Folly into a trot, turned round to see whether his pupils were all right.

He didn't like teaching – not like Pat did, anyway. He would rather be jumping, schooling a young horse, even sometimes grooming or cleaning tack. Sometimes teaching bored him; because of this, Pat took out and instructed a higher percentage of pupils, while he spent more time with Tornado, until now she whinnied whenever he approached.

He thought about her now, riding through the woods. Tomorrow one of them would ride her round the yard led by the other. 'Will she do anything?' he wondered. 'Will she ever be quiet enough for pupils?' He imagined himself riding her in front of a class. 'She will walk freely,' he thought, 'but with splendid carriage. There is something proud about her, something still untamed.'

The air seemed closer still, one could almost smell thunder. No one was talking. The sky had turned darker and a light breeze had come from nowhere; presumably to herald the thunder, thought David.

"I think it's going to rain, don't you, Dave?" called Julia.

He didn't like being called Dave; even his family didn't call him that, and he hardly knew Julia.

37

"I shouldn't be surprised," he called back, and again he turned in his saddle to see that everyone was safe and sitting properly.

They came presently to what Pat and David had always called the Vale. It was a long, open stretch of grass between the trees. The ground was always soft and springy there, and smelt of pine needles and of thyme.

As soon as they reached this place, John said, "Oh, how wizard! Now we can canter."

"How super!" exclaimed Julia.

David had a moment of panic. They couldn't all canter. He didn't know what to do. He stared at Folly's ears before he said, "Peter's not ready to canter. How do you feel about it, Judy?"

He had to make a plan. John and Julia will have to stay behind and canter to catch us up, he decided. He didn't like the idea, but what else could he do?

"Can't I canter?" asked Peter, suddenly coming to life, smiling at David with eyes as brown as his own.

"Not yet. You're only just off the lead," David replied.

"I've cantered before," said Judy, but David was remembering that she was nervous; any little thing could put her off riding for ever. He said:

"John and Julia, stay behind. When we're halfway up the Vale, you can canter and catch us up."

"Oke," replied John.

"I'd rather come along with you," said Julia, wrinkling up her nose, which was a little large for her face.

They set off along the Vale. John waited behind on an impatient Suzy, and David suddenly realised that Suzy had probably never waited behind before. He felt very tense leading the way; he had an awful sense of foreboding. Folly wanted to canter; she jogged and blew through her nostrils, so that Julia said:

"She looks like a charger."

"I wish I could canter," muttered Judy.

And then it happened – just as John had started to canter along the Vale on an excited Suzy. A dog came out of

38

the undergrowth with a rush and a bark, the ponies leapt forward and a gun went off. David jumped himself, everyone jumped, and then the ponies were tearing past David, kicking up the springy turf, while he screamed, "Sit down in your saddles. Pull on the reins," and prayed: "God, make them stop."

Suzy came past him last. He tried to grab her rein, to block her path, but failed. John was leaning forward clutching Suzy's handsome skewbald neck. His heels were against her sides, unintentionally urging her faster.

Further ahead Judy was screaming. Peter was falling off slowly, holding on till the last moment. For a second he seemed entangled with Sinbad's hoofs; then the black pony was cantering on and he was lying still on the springy turf among the pine needles, amid the smell of thyme. Julia had lost her reins; she had outdistanced everybody; in a few minutes she had left the Vale.

'Where will they go? Will they gallop home? Will they be killed by traffic on the main road? Will they tear across the Common, scaring picnickers, ruining our reputation for ever?' wondered David, stiff with fright, his heart suddenly numb as he dismounted and bent down to look at Peter.

It was very still in the Vale now; nothing seemed to stir. The dog had vanished after the runaway ponies in a wild ecstasy of excitement, still yapping doubtless, but too far away for David to hear.

Peter gave a groan and sat up, his face white under his crash cap – or was it always white? David wondered.

"I'm all right. But where are the others? Where's Mistletoe?" he asked.

"They've all gone," David answered, while Peter stood up and said, "Oh, I shall have to walk home then," in aggrieved accents.

"You can ride Folly," replied David, thinking: 'I shall never catch up with them now. And what will Pat say? And what will their parents say? And will they be hurt?' he wondered, legging up Peter on to Folly, who was be-

Then the ponies were tearing past David

coming impatient, walking on along the Vale without hope, with a heart as heavy as lead, while the first crash of thunder boomed among the trees.

"It's going to rain," said Peter.

"Looks like it," agreed David.

"Do you think we'll catch them up?"

"I doubt it."

There'll be nothing left. Nobody will come to us any more, thought David, feeling such desolation of spirit that he could have wept.

"Did you see the lightning?" cried Peter.

"No."

"Do you like thunderstorms?"

"No."

The little boy went on chattering gaily, while the trees started to sway in an ominous breeze and the sky darkened. Folly walked calmly now, as though she sensed a tragedy.

The first drops of rain fell, and now they were on the strip of road before the Common and there were blue scratch marks on the tarmac left by skidding hoofs and David thought: 'Supposing the ponies fall and break their knees? And John hasn't a hat. Oh, why did it have to happen? And, life is like that: nothing is perfect for long; always there is tragedy lurking round the corner.'

"Aren't they big drops?" asked Peter. "I do like Folly. She feels lovely and big after Mistletoe."

"I expect she does," said David. 'Peter will be a good rider in the end,' he thought. 'He has the right sort of nerves; but after today Judy will never ride again.'

The rain was coming down in torrents.

"I wish I had brought my mac," said Peter. Colour had come back to his face. He was all smiles now; this was his big adventure; soon he would be telling his friends about it with relish, boasting about his ride on Folly, adding a bit here and there.

And then they saw a pony and rider coming to meet them, and it was Julia. "Hullo, there," she called. "I don't

41

know where the others are. I managed to turn Swallow round."

"Jolly good," exclaimed David, trying to sound bright and managing, as though a runaway was the most ordinary thing in the world, as though it didn't worry him at all.

"Is Peter all right?" asked Julia, drawing rein, while the water from her hair dripped on her pale blue shirt.

"What?" said Peter.

"Yes. Quite," replied David.

"Did you fall off? I did. Folly's lovely," cried Peter.

"Are the others still on?" asked David, walking on along the road, seeing the Common a vivid green now that it had rained.

A crash of thunder obliterated Julia's answer; but when it had died away and the rain was coming down even thicker than before, she repeated what she had said: "Judy was still screaming; John looked like falling off any moment. I did my best, but there seemed no point in pursuing them."

It was cold comfort to David. He was drenched now, but not cold, because it was too warm for that.

"No. It's never any good chasing ponies," he agreed; and Julia smiled at him and said, "That's what I thought."

Peter had returned to his own private world. They reached the Common and saw John coming to meet them, his hair full of bracken, his face covered with blood. He can walk, anyway, thought David. But what about Judy?

"It's only my nose. I fell on it," John called, laughing, so that David's heart lifted a little and he thought: 'Perhaps everything won't be so bad after all.'

"Do you know what's happened to Judy?" David asked. John shook his head.

"I don't know where Suzy is either," he said. 'Home, I expect,' thought David, and imagined her tearing into the yard, stirrups flying – if she had any left on her saddle – mane flying, dripping with sweat. 'Poor Pat,' he thought. 'She'll be so upset,' and quickened his pace.

"Has anyone a handkerchief?" asked John.

42

Julia produced a dainty one with frilly edges. Peter came back to reality.

"Your face is covered with blood, John," he said, noticing it for the first time.

'I never really thought we were good enough to run a school,' remembered David, 'but Pat was insistent and after a time I believed her, and now this has happened and our name will be mud.'

There was no one on the Common; everyone had been driven home or indoors by the rain. The thunderstorm continued.

'Supposing Judy's badly hurt?' thought David. 'Lots of people must have heard her scream.' And he looked around for people on their doorsteps, but there was no one, so that he thought, 'Perhaps Sinbad's galloped to the Vicarage' – where he had been until they fetched him home.

John's nose had stopped bleeding. He said to Julia, "I'll keep your handkerchief until it's been to the laundry."

"I wonder where Judy is?" said Peter, as though he had just started to think about her.

They had reached the other side of the Common now. They walked along the familiar road, along which David had gone so merrily only that morning. 'I wonder if anyone has told Mum yet?' he wondered.

The thunder gave a last rumble and died away as they reached the drive and walked past the recently erected notice which proclaimed, *Elm Tree Riding School*.

There were fresh hoof-marks on the gravel.

"It looks as though the ponies have reached home, anyway," David said.

His shirt was sticking to his body, his hair plastered to his head. As quickly as it had started, it stopped raining, as though it had only come to speed the galloping ponies.

David's heart was hammering again. He felt sick. He could only think: 'Supposing Judy's badly hurt? Imagine Pat ringing for an ambulance, bandaging wounds, her chestnut hair falling over her eyes as she bent over the casualty.' And then he saw her running to meet them.

43

"Hullo," she called. "Is everyone all right? Suzy and Mistletoe and Sinbad are here."

Her chestnut hair was wet; she must have been looking for them. His heart seemed to stop beating altogether before he said, "Haven't you got Judy?"

"Judy?" cried Pat.

"Perhaps she's gone home," suggested John.

But none of them thought that as they walked on along the drive, all suddenly silent, all wondering, 'What has happened to Judy?' while overhead the dark sky lightened.

"Where can she have gone?" cried Pat.

"I don't know," David said.

"She can't just have vanished," cried Pat.

Repercussions

They put the ponies away, all of which were unhurt by their adventures. John's nose was turning blue; Peter was unmarked by his toss; Julia asked David questions incessantly.

"What shall we do?" asked Pat when at last she managed to catch him alone for a moment.

"I don't know," David replied. "I wish the pupils would go. It would be easier to think without them."

"It's terrible. Where can she be?" said Pat.

The sky had cleared completely; any moment the sun would be shining again.

"We must do something," cried Pat.

"Yes," said David, who was feeling stupidly numb again. But what? Search the Common? Ring up the police? Ring up her parents? Ring up all the local hospitals?

"She may have gone home. After all, she doesn't live very far away," Pat said.

"Perhaps we'd better telephone there first," David said

in an agony of indecision, thinking: 'We must do something. We can't just stand and talk.'

Julia came into the saddle-room with straw in her hair. "I've rubbed down Swallow for ages. I'm sure she must be dry now."

"Thank you very much. I think you ought to rush home and change. Or can I lend you a dry shirt?" asked Pat.

And all the time David was longing for action, wanting the feel of a telephone receiver between his fingers, to be running back along the road calling, "Judy, Judy." To be searching the Common, looking in the bracken and behind gorse bushes for the small girl who had disappeared screaming on Sinbad more than thirty minutes ago.

Then they all heard the swish of tyres on wet gravel and presently a large, pale green car came into view, driven by a woman with rimless glasses, dressed in a wool skirt and blouse, in spite of the heat of the day.

For a moment David thought, 'A pupil's mother.' Then he realised that he had never before seen this woman who had stopped the car in front of them all and was getting out. She had grey hair arranged in waves; fingers adorned with rings.

Pat was thinking 'Who can she be?' as the forbidding woman stood for a moment surveying them, before she opened her mouth to say, "I picked up a little girl on the Common. I don't know whether she came from Lere. She kept saying, 'The riding school,' so I thought perhaps she did."

David didn't doubt for an instant that she was the bearer of bad news. Pat looked as though she wanted to burst into tears. David thought: 'We should have been looking for Judy, and here we are just standing together in the saddle-room. What can she think of us? What has she done with Judy?'

"Yes, ma'am. She did come from here. We've been very worried about her. It's a relief to know that someone has picked her up," he said.

45

"Well, she's in the Wingfield with a compound fracture of her right arm. I suggest you get in touch with her parents," said the woman, turning towards her car as though she wanted no more to do with any of them.

"Whew!" exclaimed John.

There was a lump in David's throat. He thought: 'Poor Judy. Poor Judy. She'll never want to ride again. I've broken her nerve for ever. Why did it have to happen?'

"Poor kid," said Julia.

"What's a fracture?" asked Peter.

And now David felt flat and defeated.

"We had better ring up her mother," he said, picking up the telephone directory.

The woman turned her car and drove away without looking back at them.

"Would you like me to do it?" asked Pat.

"No. It's my job," replied David.

"I think I had better go," said Julia.

"Same here," agreed John.

They took Peter with them, and so at last Pat could turn to David and say, "Isn't it awful? You must have had a terrible time."

"She'll never ride again," replied David, finding Birch, which was Judy's surname, in the directory.

"She was bound to give up sooner or later. You know she was. She was one of those people who only need one toss to put them off, and you can't keep anyone on for ever," said Pat, leaning against the saddle-horse and looking at David with troubled blue eyes.

"It's awful just the same," replied David, dialling a number, thinking, 'What will Mrs. Birch say? I never want to take another class,' feeling sick again, wishing the day was over.

"I'm just no good. That's the fact of the matter." he said.

"What nonsense. It wasn't your fault. It was the dog's fault, not to mention the man with the gun," replied Pat, who by this time knew exactly what had happened.

46

David was through. "Hullo. Can I speak to Mrs. Birch?" he asked, and thought at the same time: 'Supposing she's out? Supposing no one knows where she is?'

But the voice which had answered was saying, "It's Mrs. Birch. Who is it speaking?"

And David cried, "It's about your daughter. I'm very sorry, she's had a toss. She fell off on the Common. She's been taken to the Wingfield with a broken arm." He felt quite limp now that it was said. Mrs. Birch had a high voice. He imagined her small, with delicate features and curly hair.

Pat was clutching his elbow.

"Oh dear, oh dear," said Mrs. Birch. "It's the riding school, isn't it?"

"She's dazed," muttered Pat.

"Yes. It's a compound fracture. I think the hospital would like you to get in touch with them," suggested David.

"Yes, yes. Of course," said Mrs. Birch, sounding older. "It's very good of you to ring up."

"I can't say how sorry we are," replied David.

"She's being terribly nice about it," muttered Pat.

Much to their relief, she didn't ask how the accident had occurred, 'though,' David thought, 'she'll know soon enough.' She thanked them for ringing her up and said:

"I'll get on to the hospital right away. It wasn't your fault. Accidents will happen, however careful one is. One must be thankful it's only a broken arm."

When David had replaced the receiver, Pat cried, "Wasn't she nice about it? She sounded a very nice person. Didn't you think so?"

"We must have met her," replied David, trying to remember the parents who had called in the beginning. But, however hard he tried, he couldn't remember Mrs. Birch.

He was beginning to feel more cheerful and thought again: 'Perhaps everything will turn out all right after all.' But, looking back afterwards, that day would always seem one of the worst in his life. Watching the ponies galloping

47

away ahead of him while the Vale rang with Judy's screams was something he would dream about at intervals for years.

Pat was beginning to wash the tack.

"Come on," she said. "It's late now; if you're much later home, your mother will think it's you who's in hospital instead of Judy."

"You must have had a fright when the ponies came into the yard," said David, finding a sponge, beginning to work, thinking: 'Thank goodness it's over.'

"Yes; it was awful," replied Pat with a shudder.

"Everyone will know soon," said David.

"If anyone saw."

"They must have done. Think of the clattering hoofs."

"But it was raining. People don't stand outside watching runaway ponies in a thunderstorm," said Pat.

'That's true,' thought David. 'Perhaps no one saw them. Perhaps no one knows.'

"It must happen to lots of riding schools, anyway. Do cheer up. You take everything so seriously," grumbled Pat.

Going home across the Common, which smelt warm and wet, David began to feel better. By the time he reached the cottage he had pushed the whole incident into the back of his mind and was thinking about Tornado again.

"You're late. I've kept something warm for you in the oven," his mother said.

His father was outside digging the garden; he was there most evenings during the summer, and the Smiths' garden was as good as any in the village.

His mother handed David a helping of shepherd's pie. "You had a bad day, then," she said, and David thought: 'She knows. Everyone probably knows.' And his heart sank, and he saw an empty diary in a deserted saddle-room.

"Yes. Horrible. A dog ran out and then a man fired a gun. How did you know?" he asked.

"Mrs. Tout saw the ponies galloping along the road. Awful, she said it was – one girl screaming blue murder,

48

and a boy half off, and an older girl jerking at her reins and shouting instructions to the others."

And Mrs. Tout was the gossip of the village, David remembered.

"Then a lady in a big car picked up the screaming girl. Mrs. Tout saw her fall off and everything. But she didn't see you, not anywhere," his mother finished.

David started to explain. He felt weary beyond words. He thought: 'Every time I walk along the road someone will ask about it.'

'How's the little girl?' they'll ask. Or 'What happened last Wednesday? I hear some of your ponies ran away.'

But his mother was sympathetic.

She said: "These things happen, David, and people talk about them, and then in a few days they're forgotten. It's no good worrying. You can't do more than what you can. And it's obvious it wasn't your fault. You couldn't stop the dog coming out, or the man firing the gun."

"I might have stopped the ponies, though," said David, taking his plate and cup to the little scullery because he had finished.

"Well, you had your own to hold, hadn't you? And the little boy to pick up," his mother said.

He went to bed, and in the sky there seemed a million stars. He lay and looked at them and thought: 'Anyway, it's over now, and the sooner I forget it the better. What's done is done, and *it's no good crying over spilt milk.*' But he could still hear Judy's screams, and he saw Peter again lying on the grass while Mistletoe's hoofs went over him, and in his head the thunder boomed again until at last he fell asleep, and dreamed he was jumping Tornado at a show and she had fifteen faults.

But the runaway was to have its repercussions. Next morning a mother rang up and cancelled her daughter's lesson and didn't book another one.

In the afternoon, when the postman came, he brought an

envelope addressed to *The Proprietors, Elm Tree Riding School*, and Pat, who took it, cried, "David, come quickly. Here's a letter from the Headmistress," because only she addressed them like that.

"Perhaps it's good news," cried Pat, tearing the envelope open as David appeared. Then her face fell and she handed the single sheet of paper to David.

He read:

> *Dear Miss Lewisham, – We have been into the matter of your teaching riding to the girls here very thoroughly, and have come to the conclusion that you and your partner are rather young to accept so much responsibility.*
>
> > *Yours truly,*
> > *C. Matthews,*
> > *Headmistress.*

It had been posted that morning.

"Now, don't jump to silly conclusions," cried Pat when David looked at the postmark. "It was nothing to do with yesterday. How could she have heard so soon?"

"Someone could have rung up. She could have written straight away."

"She could have, but I bet she didn't," cried Pat furiously, so that David knew she was disappointed – more so than himself, because he had never wanted to teach the girls.

"Bang goes thirty or forty pounds a term," cried Pat, picking up a brush. "Why does age matter so? There are lots of people of sixty who are completely incompetent; there are people who take rides when they're drunk."

David said nothing, because he couldn't help thinking: 'It's my fault.' And he felt mean because he didn't care as much as Pat.

He found a brush and started to groom Tornado, and saw that the trees in the field were beginning to change colour and thought: 'We'll soon be hunting now.' "Would you like to hunt?" he asked Tornado, who turned and nuzzled his hair.

The holidays ended. Pat returned to school, leaving David to run their business alone. October came mellow, gold and lovely; the ponies' coats began to grow; new pupils came. Judy's fall and the runaway ponies were nearly forgotten.

The week-ends were always full of pupils now, even when it rained. During the weekdays there were three adults who came each on a different day: grey-haired, elderly Miss Adams, who looked after her invalid father; Mrs. Poole, who was young, with three children; and a light, cheerful American airman from Ohio. Otherwise David had all the week for Tornado, and for hunting Folly if hounds met near.

Except for Tornado, time seemed to stand still during October and November. There was no milestone reached to be remembered afterwards, no sudden achievement; day followed day, each much the same as the other. But Tornado progressed until he was riding her alone and discovering that her stride was as long and low as he had expected, her head carriage high, her temperament fiery, so that often he found himself thinking: 'She'll never make a show jumper. She'll never be calm enough.' She still shied a lot and David soon realised that she wasn't everybody's ride. 'And she'll be crazy hunting,' he reflected, and would wonder whether she would ever make anything, whether they'd ever sell her or whether his forty pounds was lost for ever.

His mother was encouraging. "Give her time," she'd say. "You haven't had her for so long."

But the Huntsman and Mr. Austin, the stud groom, weren't at all optimistic.

"I've seen them like that before. You'll never make anything of her," the Huntsman said.

51

"Try to sell her for her looks. You'll never sell her for anything else," Mr. Austin said, and David, who had little confidence in himself, would think, 'They're probably right.'

Once a week, on Sunday evening, he would laboriously write to Pat. She always replied enthusiastically:

Don't worry so much. Tornado's going to be all right. I'm glad to hear you've got another new pupil. We'll need another pony soon. I never thought we'd do so well, did you?

Or:

I'm glad to hear Tornado jumps so well on the lunge. She'll probably end up a champion point-to-pointer.

David, whose letters were full of facts and figures, was often irritated by Pat's replies. She nearly always ignored his sums or dismissed them with some frivolous comment, so he came to the conclusion that, because she had never been troubled over money, she didn't understand it.

In November he clipped Swallow and Folly. By December Tornado was jumping four feet on the lunge, could canter on either leg quietly round the school, could rein back straight with her head in the right place, turn on the forehand and haunches and trot over cavaletti. But she was still a hot ride, still shied a lot and was very erratic – one day raising David's hopes to the skies, only to dash them the next by a fit of temperament.

So the holidays came again. Pat returned a little taller, changed her hair style, talked about dances and for the first day or two seemed a stranger to David, who was still only interested in horses and hadn't changed at all.

She hurried round the stables commenting on all the horses, crying, "Doesn't Tornado look ravishing? Oh, you've clipped Swallow. Hurray! They all look much smaller somehow. I feel as though I've been away for years."

David, offended, wondered whether she had ever bothered to read his letters. He had been cleaning out the boxes when she arrived and stood awkwardly holding a broom listening to her exclamations, thinking 'She's changed' with a sinking heart.

But presently all was normal again. Pat rode Tornado, who was nervous and ill at ease with a strange rider in the saddle, so that Pat said, "I think she's improved enormously, but she's definitely a one-man mare, isn't she? I mean, she doesn't like me at all."

"I expect it's because I've ridden her all along. She'll soon get used to you," David said.

But Tornado remained a one-man mare, and often David wondered what they would do with her eventually, for it seemed obvious that she would never make a tip-top show jumper; nor was she cut out to be a hunter. Her head looking over the loose box door would pull at his heart strings and he would think, 'How shall we ever sell her?' Imagine her walking up the ramp of a horse-box looking back at him reproachfully, seeming to say, "I thought you were a friend, my only friend, and now you've sold me."

'I'm just being sentimental,' David would tell himself. To get on, one must have a core of hardness. One can't ruin one's business for a horse.

Pat didn't ride Tornado again. On a cold December day they hacked to a meet on Tornado and Swallow behind hounds. It was the first cold day and there was still frost on the grass and hedges when they left the stables with hounds gay in front of them, Tornado dancing and prancing with excitement, Swallow calm but for the thrill shining in her eyes.

"Keep that mare away from my hounds, David," Bert the Huntsman called over his shoulder.

"Okay. But she doesn't kick," David said.

"You never know," Bert replied. "Not with that sort of mare."

Tornado had become a joke between them. They laughed now, and David said, "She'll be all right. You've got a grudge because she's better-looking than any of yours."

53

The meet was outside the Four Feathers, a well-known old coaching inn. There were already cars outside when they arrived, and the sound of laughter from within.

Tornado didn't want to go anywhere near. She stood still in the middle of the road, her forelegs straddled, her eyes bulging, and as Bert rode on with the pack David could hear him laughing.

"Can't you hit her or anything?" asked Pat.

"She's frightened. After all, it's her first meet."

"Well, I'm going on," said Pat, riding away elegant in her black coat, her hair encased in a net.

At last Tornado moved forward with a dash, more because there was a car on her heels than anything else.

Several Pony Club members called "Hullo" to David. He and Pat had scraped through their A Test during the summer, David with the better marks, but in spite of that David never felt really at home with the Pony Club members; he always had the feeling they were laughing at him.

He called back "Hullo," and Merry, who long ago Sinbad had kicked on the ankle, came across and said, "What's that you're riding?"

He told her about Tornado, though it was difficult enough with the bay mare turning all ways, pawing the road with all her hoofs in turn, snorting at people and hounds, shying at bicycles and prams.

"I know. The one you bought at the sale. Well, you seem to have broken her, anyway," Merry said.

"Have people been talking about her, then?" asked David.

"Oh, yes. She was talked about before you had her. No one handled her till she was seven. She ran wild in fifty acres, and her mother killed another horse. Oh, and her father wouldn't be touched on his right side at all. I'm surprised you are on her at all. People were beginning to despair, you know. I suppose you wouldn't have bought her if you had known all that," finished Merry.

"I don't know. It's difficult to say," replied David slowly.

"Come on. Hounds are moving off."

He hadn't meant to follow, but he rode on with Merry, who was small and dark, with tiny bones and grey eyes.

"I don't seem to have seen you for ages. You run a school with Pat, don't you? I'm just home for the holidays. I've got two more years. Awful, isn't it?"

"What then?"

"I suppose some beastly career or a job or something," Merry said.

They had come to a gate. There was a hold-up while someone opened it. Tornado was behaving like a rocking horse.

"She looks lovely, but awful too," Merry said.

Pat was somewhere in front. They all cantered to the first covert and Tornado threw her head about and arched her back and stiffened her neck until it felt like a very straight piece of steel.

"Is this her first hunt?" asked Merry.

"Yes. I didn't really mean to follow."

"Well, you're here now," Merry said.

"For better or worse."

She wouldn't stand at covert side, but pawed and dug and once stood straight up on end, so that several people gasped and someone said, "Is she safe?"

"He's mad bringing her out like that," a tall woman on a fourteen-two pony replied, while the first hound spoke and David thought, 'I must go home in a moment. I'll just wait another second to see whether anything happens.'

But now a second hound was speaking, then a third, a fourth, so that David, who knew most of the hounds, could think, 'That's Rapture. That's Whynot,' until the whole pack seemed to be speaking and Bert was blowing the "Gone away," and someone was hollering and all David's good resolutions seemed to have gone with the wind. And now they were galloping on, and in the distance there were hills sloping gently amid stone walls.

There was a scrum at a gate, a field of grass, trees, a stretch of woodland, more grass before a jump of slip rails.

55

Someone said, "Is she safe?"

'I must go home in a moment. I must go home,' thought David, crossing the first field, hitting his knee on a tree, seeing the rails ahead, thinking, 'She can do them if she'll go slowly enough.'

He could see Pat was over. Merry grinned at him over her shoulder before she jumped them on her chestnut. He rode Tornado as slowly as he dared and she stood right back and had jumped before he had time to think and his heart was singing as he galloped on.

Presently there was plough – light, because there had been little rain – and then a wall which Tornado took in her stride. 'I must go home in a moment. I must go home,' thought David, noticing that Tornado's neck was already flecked with lather, that her nostrils and eyes were wide with excitement.

They came to a hill with hounds running directly in front of them, close together in full cry.

"How's she going?" called Merry.

"Oaky," called David, and saw Pat look back over her shoulder.

They came to a long, flat field and more stone walls. Then hounds checked on the edge of a copse.

"They're running like smoke today," said a man who looked as though he spent half his life in the hunting field.

"I'm going home," David said.

"About time too," called Colonel Lewisham. "You've had that mare out too long already. It's her first time, isn't it?"

"Yes, sir," replied David, suddenly downcast, turning Tornado, who wouldn't stand, who was sweating and trembling in every limb, thinking, 'I've probably ruined her for life.'

Pat turned and waved. Merry said, "Going home? Goodbye, then."

It was sad to turn, to ride away just as hounds picked up the line again, to hear them hunting and ride in the opposite direction.

Tornado was still trembling, and 'She won't stop for

hours,' David thought. She wouldn't walk, and when David told her to trot she would only canter sideways. 'She's behind the bit,' he thought, driving her with his legs, remembering how friendly Merry had been, how beautifully Tornado had jumped.

They came to the road, and now she trotted and the frost had thawed and the sun came out. There are only five days to Christmas, remembered David. He had bought Pat a book. Now he decided to send Merry a card. 'And if I've ruined Tornado, I've ruined her,' he thought, letting his spirits rise a little. And then he thought, 'I know what she'll do. She'll one-day event,' and he felt excitement rising in him, and thought, 'She's bold; she has lots of scope; she's handy,' and he wished that Pat was beside him so that he could turn and say, "I've had a brain-wave. Why shouldn't Tornado one-day event?"

But she wasn't there, so he rode on making plans, dreaming of success, wondering whether Tornado would ever be calm enough for dressage.

'I shall have to work on her, that's all,' he thought, counting up the months till April on his fingers, pushing Tornado on, remembering he had three pupils at two-thirty.

Merry

Christmas was wet. David and Pat stayed in their respective homes, only meeting in the morning and evening at the stables. Pat gave David a large and expensive pigskin wallet. His mother gave him a tie-pin, his father a book token, his brothers book-ends, his sister a yellow scarf. He and Pat had received twenty Christmas cards from pupils which now adorned the saddle-room. He had half a dozen of his own besides, including a grey horse from Merry.

On Boxing Day Pat escorted four pupils hunting, while David stayed behind, did the boxes, swept the yard and schooled Tornado.

He had discussed her prospects as a one-day event horse with Pat.

"Yes. I suppose she might be all right," Pat said, "if she isn't too hot. But if she starts tearing at her fences you'll break your neck. They're all solid, you know."

David knew about one-day events. He felt annoyed with Pat. 'She doesn't seem to think I know anything at all.' he thought.

"I'm quite aware of that," he replied.

"It's worth trying, anyway," Pat said.

"You don't like her much, do you?" asked David.

"I think she's silly, and I never have cared for silly horses. I haven't got your patience," replied Pat after a moment.

"I'm sorry she's here, then, eating her head off," David said stiffly.

"Oh, don't be silly. Why are you so touchy? You know I didn't mean that."

It was like that; it wasn't like it used to be any more; any little thing seemed to start an argument, until they were both on the offensive. 'I expect it's my fault,' David thought now. 'I probably am touchy, but Pat isn't like she used to be. She's grown up now, and she hardly spoke to me last time we hunted together, and was cross when Tornado was silly at the meet.'

Later Pat rode away down the drive with the pupils and David turned to Tornado, and the day ahead looked very long.

He groomed her and schooled her and, because suddenly he was depressed, she seemed to have no future and the idea of her ever one-day-eventing seemed nothing but an impulsive idea which was better dismissed.

Putting hay and water in the boxes which awaited the hunters' return, he thought, this is the dullest Boxing Day I've ever spent, and couldn't help feeling that he had taken the wrong road somewhere, that his life was travelling very fast in the wrong direction.

But when in the evening the ponies returned, muddy and

tired, and the yard was full of voices, and Pat was saying, "I wish you had been with us. We had a lovely day," his spirits rose again, and he thought: 'These children would most likely never have hunted but for us, lots of children learn to ride simply because we're here,' and that made his life suddenly seem worth while.

Three days after Boxing Day the Pony Club dance was held. David hadn't meant to go. But at the last moment Merry came riding round to the cottage on her chestnut pony in the dark.

She knocked at the door and Mrs. Smith, opening it, cried "David, there's a girl on a pony outside."

David thought, 'Who can it be? Something must be wrong.' Awful visions leapt to view – the stables on fire, Folly dying of colic, a box door swinging in the wind while one of the ponies galloped into a lorry on the main road. But when he saw that it was Merry, he only thought, 'What can she want?'

"I'm sorry to bother you like this," she said, and he noticed that she was wearing a riding mac which seemed to cover all of her but her ears and her nose.

She didn't say any more, so he said, "That's all right. I can't ask you in because of your pony."

"It's about the dance. I thought you were going with Pat, but I hear you're not, so . . . well, I just wondered whether we could go together. That was all," she finished, looking away from him down the road.

He hadn't wanted to go to the dance; he didn't like dances; then Pat had been asked to join a party and that had seemed to settle the question, because it hadn't dawned on him he might go with someone else. Now he stood staring, like Merry, down the road, trying to make up his mind.

"You know I haven't any evening clothes," he said at last.

"Well, I don't care if you haven't," she replied. "I

wasn't thinking of wearing a long frock or anything. I haven't got one, anyway."

"I'm a very bad dancer too," he said next.

"So am I," cried Merry, beginning to laugh. And suddenly, standing there laughing with Merry, he thought it would be fun to go.

"Well, thank you very much," he said.

"Oh, hurray! You're coming, then. Mummy will get the tickets. I'd better go. I'm not supposed to be out so late," said Merry, mounting her chestnut.

She turned to wave as she rode away down the road.

He went back into the cottage.

"What a nice young lady," his mother said.

"We're going to the Pony Club dance together," he told her.

It was the first time he had been to a dance for four years. He thought, 'What shall I wear? Shall I be able to dance?'

"I must look through your things, then," his mother said, unable to keep the gladness from her voice.

He had a sort of high tea with Merry and her parents before the dance. They lived in a small, Georgian house, and the pony, which was called Dreamy, had his loose box directly opposite the back door. Merry was wearing a checked tafetta frock, full-skirted, bare on the shoulders; David wore his one and only suit.

People were already dancing when they arrived at the hall where it was held. David hadn't told Pat that he was escorting Merry, because he had wanted to give her a surprise.

Now she came across and said, "I didn't know you were coming. Why didn't you tell me?"

Merry was upstairs taking off her coat.

"I thought I would give you a surprise," he said.

"Have you come by yourself?"

He explained about Merry as she came back across the floor. He suddenly felt three years older, no longer afraid of dancing, of what people might think, no longer minding that he hadn't evening clothes.

Halfway through the evening, the Secretary of the Pony Club came across to David and Merry as they sat together at a table drinking orange juice and talking about the other members.

"Oh, David, I'm wondering whether you can help us out. It's about the trip to the circus. You had a card, didn't you? Someone's let us down and we need a capable person to help look after some of the younger children," said the Secretary.

David thought, 'I'm not capable.' "What does it entail?" he asked.

"Marshalling them together, counting them – that sort of thing. There's usually a couple of mothers on the 'bus, so it's not very difficult."

"I won't be the only person, will I?" he asked. "I mean there will be other people in charge?"

"Good lord, yes."

"It's the day after tomorrow, isn't it?" he asked, trying to remember.

"That's right."

"Are you going?" he asked Merry.

"No. My funds won't run to it," she said.

"What about if I get the ticket?" asked David.

"I'm afraid they're all booked," said the Secretary.

He said he would go, and at the same time felt it was the wrong decision, because he had never been to London before, nor to a circus.

He turned to Merry and said, "It's rather frightening, isn't it? I mean, I don't know half the children. What do you think I'm supposed to do?"

"Keep them away from wild animals, count them occasionally, I suppose."

"Why on earth did she choose me?"

"I suppose she thinks you're capable."

"More likely no one else would take it on. Come on, let's dance," he said.

The decision haunted him.

"Supposing I lose some of the children?" he asked Pat the next day.

"Why should you? You always make such mountains out of molehills," complained Pat, who hadn't enjoyed the dance.

"Wouldn't you like to go instead of me?"

"No, thank you. Anyway, I wasn't asked," she said.

He was still lit up by the dance. He had enjoyed every moment of it.

"I'm going to go to lots of dances now," he told Pat once.

His mother had been delighted when he had returned at one in the morning. She had gone to bed, but she hadn't slept. She made him tea and heard about it all and said, "Now don't start worrying about the circus. They wouldn't have asked you if you couldn't do it," and "Now you know you can dance all right, you can go to lots of them. Get out and enjoy yourself a bit. You're only young once."

The day after the dance it snowed.

Looking at it gloomily, Pat said, "Let's hope it doesn't go on and on. We don't want the ponies eating their heads off and not doing any work."

It was a fear very near to them both. Six weeks of snow and ice could ruin their business: they both knew that.

But today David was optimistic.

"It's not cold enough for much; it'll soon turn to rain," he said.

There wasn't enough snow to stop them riding, though two pupils put off. They took out what remained of the class through woods where the snow was thawing as it fell and across fields where you could still see the grass, though here and there the flakes, which fell silently as though from another world, were lying.

A boy called Timothy fell off; but Mistletoe stood waiting for him, and he laughed and said, "That's the third. I'm getting on, aren't I?"

They returned with cold hands and feet and pink faces. Already the snow in the drive was turning to slush.

"You'll see, it won't last," said David, talking like his mother.

It didn't last, but the next day there was still snow in the air, and David, rising early, looking out of his window, remembering that he had to escort a 'bus load of children to the circus, thought, 'I hope it stays fine. If it snows, it'll be cold coming home; the roads might get blocked; anything could happen.'

Pat was mucking out when he arrived at the stables.

"You shouldn't have bothered to come down. You know it's your day off," she said.

"Only from eight o'clock," he replied.

It was bitterly cold, raw and damp; dawn had come dark and forbidding. Pat's hands were cold, the handles of the brooms and forks were wet. Folly's coat stood on end, so that David said, "I think she could do with another rug."

"I don't believe we've got any more," replied Pat.

"Oh, well, Mum's probably got an old one somewhere which will do," said David.

Walking home while the first flakes of snow were falling, David thought, 'I need a bike,' and resolved to ask his brother John what he had done with his now he had a car. While he dressed, his mother made him sandwiches to eat in the 'bus.

The cottage was warm and smelt of the pastry cooking in the oven.

"Your shoes could do with a spot of polish," his mother said.

When he was ready, he walked to the end of Church Lane and waited for the Secretary, who was to drive him to the town from which the 'bus was starting.

It wasn't snowing in earnest even now, though the sky looked full to the brim with it.

David imagined the 'buses coming home at night, their headlights lighting up the white roads; then the Secretary drew up in her grey brake and said, "Hop in, David."

There was tack in the back and a small girl with plaits called Jean.

64

"She's in your 'bus," the Secretary said.

He smiled at Jean and asked, "Is this your first circus?" and thought, 'She doesn't look any trouble. Everything's going to be all right.'

Jean nodded, and he said, "Mine too."

"Not really?" asked the Secretary.

"Yes."

The snow was falling faster now. "Not very nice, is it?" asked David.

"The forecast's good," said the Secretary.

It wasn't lying in the town, except on roofs and chimneys and the tops of trees.

"It probably isn't snowing at all in London," said the Secretary.

The 'buses were waiting close to the market, red and gaudy, already half full of children.

Several people called, "Hullo, David," and, stepping out into the street, he couldn't help feeling what a long way he had travelled from the little boy who had had no friends, no pony of his own, who had been awkward and left out, and sometimes despaired of ever being able to ride.

Pony Club 'Bus

The snow was thawing on the roads as the four 'buses moved off towards London. David sat beside a boy called Michael, feeling alone and responsible because after all there was no grown-up – only himself – to look after the thirty-one children. The 'buses started in convoy, but gradually they lost one another, and David wished that Pat had come, while the younger children laughed, and a fifteen-year-old boy lit a cigarette.

'What shall I do with them at the circus? How shall I keep them together?' wondered David, clutching the tickets he had been given. The Secretary had apologised.

"I'm sorry. I thought Mrs. Adams was coming," she had said. "But really there's nothing to it. Keep with the other 'buses and you'll be all right."

And here they were travelling to London without another 'bus in sight.

"Do you think it will stop snowing?" Michael asked.

"Can we go to the fun-fair afterwards?" asked a girl with plaits.

"I think it's going to go on snowing all day," said David, "And we'll think about the fun-fair when the time comes."

'If only I had been before,' he thought.

"Miss Jones let us go last year," cried a small boy.

"Yes. She did," chimed in the girl.

And now the snow was falling faster and the driver turned to David and said, "Rotten day."

"Yes. Awful," he agreed and thought, 'Supposing it goes on for weeks and weeks?' and saw that they had reached High Wycombe.

They came to London, to the circus ground, and to David's relief the other 'buses were lined up, the occupants still inside awaiting the arrival of his 'bus. They went into the arena together and David thought again, 'Everything's going to be all right.' Everyone was laughing and talking. The three adults present had counted the children. For the moment David felt free and could look forward to the circus without anxiety.

There were lions, performing dogs, beautiful Arab horses, clowns, elephants large and gentle.

One act followed another, and so enraptured were the children that the falling snow outside was forgotten.

But when the last act was finished and David's children had been to the fun-fair, been lost, re-counted again and again, until at last they were all there together by the ticket office, they could see that it had never stopped snowing. They ran to the 'bus park shivering, and were greeted by the drivers, who stood, their coat collars turned up, stamping their feet in the snow.

"What an evening," the drivers said. And "It won't be much of a drive back."

The adults present counted the children again. They clambered back into their 'buses. David nodded to his driver. For a moment the 'bus wheels skidded, then they were out of the park driving through London, and here the roads were wet with melting snow.

In the 'bus the lights were on. Twilight had come soon, snow darkened the windows.

"I hope it won't go on and on snowing. We'll get hardly any riding these hols. if it does," said Michael.

"I shall go tobogganing," someone said. For the moment the 'bus was their own private world.

'And is it snowing at home?' David was wondering, and 'Has Pat ridden Tornado?' and there was a sudden empty feeling in his stomach because if it went on snowing till March Pat and he could well be bankrupt, 'And what would my mother think then?' he wondered. 'And how many people would say, "I told you so"?'

They came to the end of London and there were no more lamp-posts, only endless miles of white road, falling snow, the sudden silence of a deserted evening. Somewhere in the maze of London streets, among the traffic lights and traffic, the 'buses had separated again, until now their 'bus travelled almost alone along the dual carriage-way leading out of London.

A brother and sister sitting together in the seat behind the driver started to sing, and gradually other people joined in until they were all singing *She'll be Coming Round the Mountain. Ten Green Bottles, This Man went to Mow*. Singing, most of them could forget the snow, but David could sense how slowly they were travelling, and where before the roads had been covered with gravel they were now covered with snow.

They had eaten at the circus, but presently sweets and

chocolates started to appear and for the moment the singing stopped.

"The road's pretty skiddy," said the driver, changing into second gear, putting out his hand before he passed a small car parked on the roadside.

"Do you think we'll make it?" David asked.

"Oh, we should be all right. But I won't promise at what time," the driver said.

The singing started again. David lost all sense of time, until presently he had no idea how far they had travelled. Two of the smaller children were asleep, their heads tucked into the corners of their seats. Most people were singing:

> *There were kippers, kippers,*
> *Smelling like father's slippers,*
> *In the quartermaster's stores. . . .*

There was a sudden rush of lights. High Wycombe, thought David with a sense of relief.

"Won't be so long now, mate," the driver said.

David thought of home, of a meal waiting for him in the oven.

> *There was cheese, cheese,*

sang the occupants of the 'bus.

There were no more lights; just a long, slippery hill and falling snow. The driver changed down.

"What we need is chains," he said.

They took the hill very slowly, so that sometimes they seemed to be hardly moving at all.

The singing continued:

> *There was flour, flour,*
> *Smelling like milk gone sour,*
> *In the quartermaster's stores . . .*

sang the children.

They topped the hill at last. The driver lit a cigarette as he drove on. A lorry passed, a car with the clinking noise of chains. 'We seem to have been travelling for hours and hours,' thought David. 'Will dozens of parents be ringing up the Secretary asking where their children are?'

The 'bus was travelling faster now; there was nothing in sight; the road was all theirs.

> *There was butter, butter,*
> *Looking like the gutter,*

sang the children.

David felt the 'bus swerve, felt the driver's foot on the brake, and the first awful sensation of a skid. He saw the shape of a corner, the verge, a tree. He thought, 'We're skidding. We're going to hit the tree,' felt a sudden rush of fear before he was thrown forward against the driver's seat, and heard the crash of metal against wood and the tinkling of glass. . . .

He must have been out for ten seconds before he was picking himself up, glancing round the 'bus, crying, "Is everyone all right?"

The driver was sitting upright in his seat wedged against the steering wheel. There was something unnatural about the straightness of his back which made David shudder. The lights had gone out. The floor was at an angle of forty-five degrees. Someone cried, "I'm all right. Isn't there a light?" And the children began to talk and someone was crying, "Oh, my head." And at the back a small voice was moaning.

It was all like a hideous nightmare to David as he felt his way to the side of the 'bus, and managed to pull up a couple of window blinds. They were sideways against a tree. Outside it was still snowing. 'This is a night I shall never forget,' thought David before he said, "Everyone who can, stand up, please, but don't step on anyone else." He saw that his right hand was bleeding, but without interest. For the moment it didn't seem to belong to him; it was simply something which would have to be seen to later.

There was a little light in the 'bus now; David could see children picking themselves up. A little girl started to giggle. A boy said, "Whew!" Someone asked, "What did we hit? A tree?"

The driver remained motionless, like a dummy propped against the steering wheel.

The door of the 'bus was buckled in.

"I think we'll be able to get out of the emergency door," Michael said.

No one was giggling now. They had all seen the driver. And there were two children who hadn't moved from where they were, and a small boy crumpled on the floor.

Nearly all the windows were smashed. Somewhere far away an owl was hooting, which seemed somehow to add to the disaster and to the sense of remoteness which hung over everything.

"Anyone done first aid?" asked David and a tall girl called Pamela stepped forward.

"Some of us had better go for help, hadn't we?" asked Michael.

The driver was knocked out; so were the children still in their seats and the little boy on the floor. No one had severed an artery, no one must be moved, Pamela told them, while Michael and David managed to wrench the emergency door open, so that presently all but the hurt were standing on the verge with snow falling fast

David's teeth were chattering and two of the younger children were crying.

"Everyone must try to keep warm," said Pamela.

"There must be a house somewhere near," cried David, but he could see now that on each side of them were woods, and nothing seemed to move but the snow and the tops of the trees.

"I wonder where the other 'buses are," someone said.

"I'll go one way. You go the other," David told Michael.

"The rest of you had better climb back into the 'bus and try to keep warm."

"What about money? One of us might find a callbox," suggested Michael.

They collected together some pennies before they each set off in a different direction down the road, and as David walked his cut hand left a trail of blood in the snow.

'It was so sudden, but I suppose accidents always are,' thought David, walking along the road, which looked humbler and narrower beneath its covering of snow. 'How badly is the driver hurt?' he wondered, quickening his pace, wondering whether the man had a wife and children waiting for him at home.

He came at last to the end of the woods and the road seemed to stretch on and on between white fields. The snow had come over the tops of his shoes; his trouser turn-ups were full of it. And then he saw a house and started to run and to pray that it was on the telephone, and to imagine help – blankets, thermoses of hot tea, an ambulance.

For a time he thought he would never reach the house. It remained simply a roof with smoking chimney in the distance. Then at last he could see its shape – twin gables, walls set square, a porch which jutted into the garden.

The last piece of road was uphill; when he stood at last jangling the front-door bell he seemed to have no breath left. He could feel his heart pounding against his ribs; his hand had stopped bleeding. He thought, 'Supposing they're out? Supposing it's empty? Why did all this ever have to happen?' He felt suddenly very alone standing there in the porch. 'If no one comes, what do I do?' he thought. But now he could hear footsteps and presently a light was switched on and David began to shout, "There's been an accident, a crash. We need help."

The footsteps moved more quickly then, and a man's voice started to talk, and David called, "Are you on the telephone?"

Minutes later the front door was opened and David faced

71

a man in flannel trousers, bedroom slippers, a rumpled shirt.

"What's happened? We haven't heard anything," he said.

"It's back along the road. Our 'bus hit a tree. There's several people hurt," David replied.

"You want an ambulance, then. I'll 'phone." David followed the man into the house.

A woman appeared and the man said, "We'll need lots of tea, Maisie, and some blankets."

"You've cut your hand," she said, looking at David.

'Everything is taking hours. I suppose it always does,' David thought. "It's nothing," he said, looking at his hand, which had started to bleed again.

Five minutes later the three of them were driving slowly back along the road armed with thermoses, cups, coats and blankets.

It had stopped snowing. The sky was beginning to clear.

"Poor kids. What club did you say you belonged to?" Maisie asked.

There was a battered car parked by the 'bus.

People began to wave and shout as David and his rescue party appeared.

"The driver's come to," someone called, seeing David. "But he's delirious or something."

A strange man was holding the driver by the arm. "What we need is an ambulance," he said.

"There's one coming," replied David, stepping out into the snow, asking, "Is Michael back yet?"

"Here he comes," cried Pamela, and there was Michael hurrying along the road with two men, one on each side.

The driver was talking nonsense. Without his cap, he was balder and looked older than he had before.

The two small girls who had been unconscious were sitting on a seat. Maisie gave them tea with plenty of sugar. David put blankets round them.

The small boy was still lying on the floor. No one had dared touch him. He looked small and pathetic; someone had lain a coat across his shoulders; now David replaced it with a rug.

The two men Michael had brought weren't much use. The man with the battered car had stopped when he saw the 'bus, and asked whether he could help. It was very cold now that it had stopped snowing. Maisie had brought bandages; now she did up David's hand.

Then the ambulance came. The two men who came with it took charge of the driver and examined the small boy.

"He's given his head a nasty bash, but there's nothing else wrong," they said, and they put the boy on the stretcher.

Before they left they said, "What about the rest of you? How are you going to get home?"

And because no one had thought about it, they all stood silently racking their brains.

"We'd better see if we can get another coach for you. I'll see they get home," announced Maisie's husband.

"You'd better come along to our place and have some food," Maisie said.

So they left the 'bus just as it was, crushed against the tree; and the girls who had been knocked unconscious rode in the car, and the rest of them walked.

There wasn't much room for them all in the house with the two gables, and they overflowed from the kitchen into the two front rooms. And now that they had left the 'bus and knew that no one was dead or dying they could talk about the accident and even laugh.

"Whew! I bet the 'bus company's fed-up," said Michael.

"The other Pony Club people must be in a stew," remarked Pamela.

Maisie's husband, who seemed to be called George, was ringing up the 'bus company.

They could all hear him talking about the accident, and the extensive details he gave made them realise that there must be some Pony Club people in the station waiting for them.

When at last George replaced the receiver, he said,

"They're sending a coach along right away. How do you all feel?"

"One of the little girls has been sick. She's lying on our bed," said Maisie.

David looked at the clock in the kitchen and cried, "Gosh! Look at the time. It's nearly midnight."

"Our parents will be in a flap," said Michael.

"You're telling me," agreed someone.

"I'm glad I'm not the Secretary," said Pamela.

"Which of you is in charge, by the way?" asked Maisie.

"I am. There was supposed to be an adult, but she didn't show up," David said.

"My Ma, incidentally," Michael added.

It seemed very warm in the house after standing in the snow outside. The kitchen was distempered cream, and there was a brand new cooker by the window.

'It seems centuries since this morning,' David thought; and imagined his parents sitting up in the cottage talking anxiously together. Some of the children were already borrowing the telephone and ringing up their parents. But the cottage wasn't on the telephone. There seemed nothing David could do but wait anxiously for the relief coach to come. 'And it'll be some time before we're home,' he thought.

"I hope we don't crash again," said the girl with fair plaits. "Mummy wanted to fetch me from here, but I said I'd rather go in a coach."

A great many of the parents weren't at home, and everyone knew that they must be anxiously waiting at the 'bus station. Some of them might even be on their way to London.

They drank tea and ate large thin slices of bread and butter, and after a time they could see that the sky had cleared and there was a moon riding high and aloof among stars.

David drew back a curtain and looked out, and so was the first to see the relief coach travelling towards them through the moonlit night.

"Here it is," he cried, turning back to the crowded room.

The children started to thank their rescuers, to find their belongings, to put on gloves and coats again.

"We ought to help wash up," said David, looking at the many dirty cups.

"Now, none of that. It's not every night there's a 'bus crash, is it, George?" Maisie asked.

Presently there was a knock at the door, and there stood a driver alarmingly like the first one.

Everyone said "Thank you" all over again before they piled into the coach which had come to take them home.

Two hours later David was walking up the garden path to the cottage, while all around cocks were heralding the approaching dawn.

There was a light still burning in the kitchen; he opened the back door and there were his parents, one on each side of the range.

"Thank God!" exclaimed his mother.

"You're all right then, son?" asked his father.

"We rang up the 'bus station. We knew there had been a crash. We've been so worried," said his mother.

He felt as though he had been away years. But he wasn't tired; he felt fully prepared to begin a new day.

"We skidded into a tree . . ." he began.

"But you must be famished. What am I thinking of . . .?" cried his mother.

'Flu

By the morning Pat had heard. David's hand had throbbed as soon as he was in bed, and at nine he was at the local doctor's surgery having it stitched.

Because of this, he was late at the stables. He arrived out of breath and apologetic. The ponies were already saddled.

"Hullo. How are you after your excitement?" called Pat.

"You've heard, then?"

"Yes. People kept ringing up last night, though why we should know about Pony Club 'buses I don't know."

"It was all rather horrible really."

"What have you done to your hand?" asked Pat.

For some reason, the accident made him feel immeasurably older. "Oh, I cut it on something – glass, I suppose," he said carelessly, as though it was nothing, though it still throbbed.

"Do you think we'll be able to ride?" Pat asked. "I saddled the ponies with an open mind."

The snow had frozen in the night; it was crisp now. The air was sharp, the sky clear and blue. 'The country must look like Switzerland,' thought David.

"I don't think the snow will ball in their hoofs," he said.

"I thought we could school quietly. I didn't ride Tornado yesterday; I didn't really have time," Pat told him.

"Do you want me to ride her?"

"I thought you'd better. I'd like to take the first class. But how about your hand?"

"It'll be all right," he said.

The first of the pupils was coming up the drive. As they bridled the ponies, David told Pat more about the crash.

"It must have been terrifying," she said.

"It happened so quickly, there wasn't time to be frightened," David replied.

Later he saddled and bridled Tornado. When he mounted her, he could feel her back was up. Almost at once his hand started to ache. She wouldn't stand still, and when he rode her down the drive the wind was so cold that it seemed to freeze his face. He thought about Pat as he turned Tornado into the road, 'Why hadn't she ridden the bay mare? Was she frightened of her? Or didn't she like her?' Tornado slipped and he guided her on to the verge. There was hardly any traffic and what came past clinked with chains.

Because suddenly David was gloomy, he tried to do sums. Were they succeeding or not, he wondered. Would

76

they ever make a success of their business? He tried to work out how much they were making now that the ponies were eating their heads off. But he soon realised that everything would depend on the future weather. It was too early to say yet whether they would prosper eventually or fail. Anything could happen during the next three crucial months.

He trotted on and on along the verge, driving Tornado into her eggbutt snaffle bridle, wondering how the small boy and the 'bus driver were, trying to cheer himself up.

By five to eleven he was back in the yard, putting a still fresh Tornado back in her box. Out of four pupils, only one came for the next class, and David took her out and tried to teach her something, and talked brightly about school and Christmas.

By the time he returned, his teeth were chattering, and Pat said, "You look awful. You shouldn't have gone out again. Go into the saddle-room and get warm."

He held his hands over the oil-stove in the saddle-room and gradually his teeth stopped chattering. His feet had been numb, but soon painfully they started to come back to life.

The solitary pupil booked up another ride and left.

"What a ghastly day. How did Tornado go?" asked Pat, coming into the saddle-room with pink cheeks and two pairs of gloves on her hands.

"Oh, okay. She was rather fresh," David answered, and wondered whether he would ever stop shivering.

"You still look awful. You must be ill or something. Perhaps you're suffering from delayed shock. What do you feel like?" Pat asked.

He felt gloomy – too gloomy to speak, too gloomy for anything. He felt a failure. He thought, 'What's the matter with me? Why can't I pull myself together?'

"I feel miserable, that's all. It's the snow and everything. Supposing it goes on for weeks and weeks?" he asked.

"Don't let's jump our fences before we come to them. I think you'd better go home," Pat said.

77

"Don't be silly; there are the lunches to do and the boxes. I'm all right," he replied.

"You don't look it. I think I'd better get a car," Pat said.

"Don't be mad. I don't need a car. I haven't lost the use of my legs."

"You look as though you have," she said.

In the end he walked home feeling gloomier each moment, until everything seemed to point to disaster so that he could have cried if only he had been younger.

When he entered the cottage his mother said, "Hullo. You're early." And then, "What's the matter? Are you feeling bad?"

He sat down and held his head in his hands.

"You shouldn't have got up so early after last night," his mother said before she put a hand on his forehead and cried, "It's bed for you, my lad. You've got a temperature. The sooner you're out of those damp clothes the better."

He found he was glad to be shepherded upstairs, to have a hot-water bottle put in his bed, a fire lit, to be fussed over and coddled, while a neighbour telephoned for the doctor.

"And I suppose you went riding with your bad hand and all," his mother complained, but her scolding voice was comforting, and now for the moment he had stopped worrying about the riding school and Pat, because there was nothing he could do now – not, anyway, until the doctor had come. The firelight flickered on the walls, and he could see the snow on the trees outside and hear a bird chirping somewhere in the thatch by his window. And now suddenly he felt quite happy lying safe and warm in his bed, and he thought, 'Tornado *will* one-day event. I know she will. And one day I shall ride for England. And the school's going to pay its way all right.' And then he saw the neighbour standing by the door saying, "He don't look too good, does he, Mrs. Smith? The lady in the surgery says Dr. Peterson will be along as soon as he can."

He dreamed that he was jumping Tornado at the Royal Windsor Show. She was hot to ride and rushed her fences, and he heard Pat say, "She'll never be any good. She's much too excitable."

Then he opened his eyes and saw Dr. Peterson standing in the doorway.

"Hullo. What's the matter with you?" he asked.

"I'm quite all right, thank you," he said, trying to out-distance the dream, which still seemed real.

The doctor took his temperature, shook his head and felt his pulse.

"You'll have to stay in bed for a few days, I'm afraid," he said, showing Mrs. Smith the thermometer.

"I don't feel very ill," David said.

When the doctor had given him an injection of penicillin and gone away, Mrs. Smith said:

"He thinks it's a bad bout of 'flu. It probably started yesterday, and hanging about in the snow last night can't have done it any good. He's heard about the two hurt in the crash. The driver was concussed; the little boy's staying in hospital under observation, but he's come round, and Dr. Peterson doesn't think there's much wrong with him."

"Oh, good. I'm glad," David said. "What's my temperature?"

"Too high to be good for you, but the injection will soon bring it down."

His mother started to tidy his bed.

"You have a nice sleep, and presently I'll bring you up some tea," she said.

"I must let Pat know."

"I'll see to that," his mother said.

He lay back and slept, and dreamed that he was riding down a long straight road with Pat, who turned to him suddenly and said, "I've decided to be a debutante after all."

He tried to smile and say, "It doesn't matter. How lovely for you," but no words came; suddenly he was speechless.

Pat came to see him.

"Don't come in," he cried, seeing her in the doorway. "You'll catch it."

"I would have caught it already if I was going to catch it," she said, coming into the room.

She was dressed in riding clothes.

"I've brought you some books. How do you feel?" she asked.

His temperature was down almost to normal, but all his bones ached, and he wasn't hungry.

"I'm miles better," he said.

She dumped the books on his bed, and he saw that there were a couple by Hammond Innes, and the rest were about riding.

"I rode Tornado first thing this morning, and she bucked me straight off," Pat said.

He was too surprised to speak for a moment; then he said, "But she hasn't bucked for ages."

"She doesn't like me, and I was in a hurry. I expect it was my fault," replied Pat without looking at David. "I mounted her again and rode her round the yard a few times. I didn't take her out, because she's so fresh, and I was afraid she would slip up and hurt herself. I thought I'd lunge her this afternoon."

"That seems a good idea," said David, wondering why Tornado had bucked, trying to imagine Pat falling off in the yard.

"You didn't hurt yourself, anyway?" he asked.

"No. Not a bit," she said.

He told her about his dream, but she didn't laugh, as he had thought she would. For an awful moment he wondered whether his dream had been a conversation ahead of time, whether he had for a moment travelled into the future, whether one day Pat would really say, "I've decided to be a debutante after all."

"You don't want to be one really?" he asked after a moment.

"A what?"

"A debutante."

80

"Of course not," Pat said.

'But supposing she changes her mind?' he thought. 'It'll be the end of the riding school. Or would it?' he wondered, and knew at the same time it would be, because he didn't care enough to carry on alone.

"Well, look after yourself," said Pat, preparing to leave.

"Thanks for coming. It's lovely to have so many books," he answered.

After she had gone, he looked at the books and thought; but his brain seemed sluggish and he came to no conclusions, beyond the fact that the riding school would be unlikely to last for ever, that teaching wasn't his *métier*, and that while he lay in bed Tornado was becoming impossible.

The next day he was allowed up for tea. The snow had thawed, outside trees dripped and there was drizzle in the air.

He wasn't hungry, but he ate a little to impress his mother.

"The doctor's coming to see you again tomorrow," she said.

He had hoped to be up the next day, to be down at the stables helping Pat; to ride Tornado, if only for half an hour.

"But I'm all right now," he said.

"He wants to give you a check-up before you start working again," she continued.

He knew it was no good arguing with his mother. Tomorrow would be just one more lost day as far as he was concerned.

"It's better to be safe than sorry," quoted his mother.

Next day the doctor pronounced him fit. "But go gently for a day or two. You've had a bad spell of 'flu, and you will get tired easily for the next few days," he said.

While David had been in bed he had read three books on riding and stable management; he had paid particular attention to instructions for getting a horse fit.

He meant to put a plan into action straight away, to waste no more time in dithering, but to enter Tornado for the next one-day event within a hundred miles.

He had always needed a goal, always some distant date, some test of his ability lying ahead. Now he was giving himself one, and for the next few months nothing would matter to him as much as Tornado's schooling, her daily exercise, her feeding and grooming.

Now his mind was made up, he felt happier. The future held hope and a new experience.

The next morning he was up early; by ten past seven he was walking across the Common while the night died and dawn came raw and grey and cold.

Fears

When David rode Tornado, who bucked once, seemed surprised that he was still on and paced out of the yard like a mustang, Pat, who was watching, called, "Well stuck on. Gosh! She looks wonderful," while David thought, 'One day she'll have a marvellous extended trot.'

Their riding school was just about paying its way. That evening they sat in the saddle-room together and sent out their December bills. They had a hay bill of twenty-two pounds waiting to be paid. They had just given the blacksmith a cheque for seven pounds.

"We'll get in quite a lot on Wednesday, anyway," said Pat.

"You mean for the children's meet?" asked David.

"Yes. Four at three guineas each is twelve pounds."

"I still think three guineas is rather a lot," David said.

It was an old argument; they could never agree on the subject.

Pat laughed now and said, "You're no business-man, David."

"I'm thinking of the poorer people," he said.

It was Monday, the ponies' day of rest.

"Later on I think we should have a sort of scholarship

class for the poorer children – in the summer, when the evenings are longer," David said.

Pat laughed. "If you like," she replied indifferently, so that David thought suddenly, 'Supposing she's really thinking of backing out?' and for a moment he felt shaky at the knees. 'If only she'll wait until I've ridden Tornado in at least one one-day event,' he thought.

"It'll be nice when the cheques start coming in," Pat said.

"I wish there were more. I think we ought to advertise that we take horses and ponies to school."

"But we haven't any more boxes," Pat replied.

"I mean when the weather's better. When most of the ponies are out," David said.

Pat had begun addressing envelopes. David turned up the oil-stove.

"You are keen on the school, aren't you?" he asked.

"Yes. Why do you keep asking?" replied Pat.

"I just wondered," he said while she continued addressing envelopes, stopping occasionally to brush back her hair.

The next day Pat had 'flu. David took out three classes. Julia helped him groom and saddle the ponies, clean the tack, put the smaller children up.

It rained. He took out the third class on Tornado, who fretted behind, but went well in front of the ponies. He had bought himself a riding mackintosh; he turned the collar up and thought about Pat; whether secretly she wanted to back out; whether her mother was persuading her to be a debutante before it was too late. He came to no conclusions. He returned gloomy, but still determined to one-day event Tornado.

Later, just before dark, he schooled Tornado over the remains of the golf-course on the Common – over the bunkers, the once-trim greens, up and down the hills, in and out of the gorse bushes. When he returned Julia was still there; she had changed the ponies' rugs, topped up their water-buckets, done the boxes. Together they put Tornado away.

Later he visited Pat, who was sitting up in bed. Her room wasn't as he remembered it. In the old days, there were picture-postcards pinned above the bed, childish ornaments on the chimney-piece. There would be copies of *Riding* and *Pony* scattered about the room. An air of untidiness would hang over everything. Now a dressing-table with triple mirror and frills had replaced the old chest of drawers, a Degas reproduction hung above the bed, on a chair lay the latest copy of *Vogue*.

David tried to ignore the change, but it all seemed to fit in with his fears.

He said, "Hullo. The front door was ajar and there didn't seem anyone about, so I just walked up."

"I'm bored stiff. Literally, I could scream with boredom," said Pat.

He told her about the three classes, how each pupil had ridden, how Peter was improving, how Joanna couldn't keep her legs still. "I think she could do with lots of riding without stirrups," he finished, and realised with an awful sense of foreboding that Pat wasn't listening.

He wanted to say, "You're not interested, are you?" but he said instead, "Don't you think so?"

"What? Oh yes, about Joanna. Oh yes, absolutely."

He had meant to tell Pat about Tornado, to say, "You should have seen her up and down the hills and over the bunkers," but suddenly there didn't seem any point any more. She wasn't interested; she didn't really care about the ponies and pupils any more.

He stood up. "I must go, or Mum will be wondering where I've got to."

"Well, thank you for coming. I was so bored. Now I feel much better," she said.

He went down the stairs, through the hall, which smelt of a mixture of dog, furniture polish, and Colonel Lewisham's tobacco, out into the dark, thinking, 'She doesn't care,' and for a moment it seemed the end of everything, because for years he had done everything with Pat, and half the ponies were hers, and the stables and paddock and field were her father's. He thought, 'I couldn't carry on alone; and I don't want to either. But why did we ever start it? Pat was so keen and now she doesn't care.'

Nothing made sense any more as he reached the road and turned left. She was enthusiastic at first, he remembered, and saw them again at the horse sale, Tornado bucking her off, the walk home.

'She hasn't said anything yet, anyway,' he consoled himself presently. 'She may not say anything for ages, perhaps never. . . .' But that he knew was wishful thinking, because *actions speak louder than words,* and Pat was clearly bored, and for the last ten days she had refused to discuss the future. And now his legs ached and he wondered what they would do with the ponies when Pat decided to give up.

From then on every day David expected the fateful news. On Wednesday he took four pupils hunting and rode Folly. The meet was at the kennels. Colonel Lewisham gave a talk. Pat appeared in ordinary clothes, looking pale and tired. Hounds found early; there was a short run across half a dozen fields before the fox went to ground in the side of a quarry. David's pupils were inclined to hang at the back of the field, but otherwise they were no trouble. The rest of the day was blank; the evening was cold and by four-thirty David was more than ready for the hack home. Once back there were the dirty ponies to settle, the boxes to do again, and at the end of it all the walk home through the dark. 'And yet,' thought David, looking at the dirty tack hanging in the saddle-room, 'I'm happy. I don't want to change this for anything on earth,' and at that moment he loved the saddle-room, the sound of munching ponies, the dark yard, the smell of hay, saddle soap and horse which hung over everything. It seemed impossible to him then that Pat could want to exchange it all for dances and parties; he patted each pony in turn, pulled Tornado's bay ears, and each moment it became more impossible until he had convinced himself that his intuition was wrong, that Pat hadn't changed except in his imagination.

He walked home feeling better, and there was a large tea waiting for him, and the kitchen was warm and familiar, and on the chimney-piece stood the cups which were like milestones in his life, each a sign pointing the way to success.

Though Pat lacked enthusiasm, she said nothing about her future plans, and David, who was afraid to ask, continued as usual, and the holidays ended and February came, as it should, with torrents of rain.

Once in January, before she went back to school, he and Merry went to the Cinema together. They saw a Western and afterwards caught a 'bus to her home and ate crumpets, tomato sandwiches and a cake she had made, in front of a blazing fire. Merry's mother was small, bustling and kind : she talked to David about the riding school, and David told her about Tornado. She was very enthusiastic.

"Merry and I will be there to watch you one-day event. Won't we, Merry?" she cried. "It must be wonderful to be so ambitious."

All through February David schooled Tornado. He hid jumps on the Common, put them on the bunkers, on the hills, at strange angles, schooled Tornado over them before hiding them once more.

Sometimes he would persuade Pat to come and watch him, and she would criticise, suggest new places for the jumps, put them up if she was near enough when Tornado knocked them down. Often she timed him with her watch and would call out, "Hurry. You're being too slow. Faster."

Sometimes she would ride Swallow to the Common, but more often she would come on foot and watch David, leaning on her father's shooting stick, looking about eighteen.

As soon as the weather improved, David set up a dressage arena. He had ridden dressage tests with the Pony Club. Once he had been nearly selected for the Inter-branch Competition, but finally he had been only reserve rider because

All through February David schooled Tornado

Folly's extended paces hadn't been good enough. Tornado was different; her extended work was the best part of her; otherwise she was too hot; she hated standing still, she was impatient to begin and impatient to finish.

March came in warm with a south-west breeze. Only a scar remained on David's hand to remind him of the 'bus crash. Suzy was going well now; during the winter her jumping had improved and she looked like becoming a promising gymkhana pony. Sinbad was the same as always; Mistletoe a little whiter. David and Pat between them had taught John to jump Folly, until now they looked a promising combination for the summer shows. The last days of the hunting season were warm and sunlit, so that people stood too long at covert-side, and sweated in their hunting clothes, and discussed their summer holidays.

The Elm Tree Riding School needed another pony, but when David mentioned the fact to Pat, she would change the subject, or simply say, "Yes. We must think about it."

"But we ought to get it before the Easter holidays. We've got enough money," he said at once, and she laughed and replied, "Well, don't let's risk a horse sale again."

"But Tornado's turned out all right," he argued. "Not that I'm suggesting a sale."

"She's a one-man mare. Don't think I'm grumbling about her. I think you've done marvels. But she's not much of a spec, is she?" asked Pat.

"But she will be," David said.

"Oh, yes. I expect so," replied Pat with a disbelieving smile, which made David furious inside, so that he said, "You never did like her, did you?"

They stood and faced one another, and for a moment it looked like a quarrel, and David was glad, because there were a lot of things he wanted to bring out into the open and this looked like a golden opportunity.

Then Pat laughed and said, "For goodness' sake, don't let's fight. I couldn't care less about the mare."

"But she's your mare too," cried David, but Pat had picked up a brush and was walking away across the yard.

"No, she isn't. She hates me," she called back over her shoulder, and somehow that seemed to finish the argument.

David stood for a moment thinking, 'Our dream has come to this,' and suddenly he wished that Merry was running the riding school with him instead of Pat.

After that his partnership with Pat started to deteriorate. They would argue over quite silly things, and once the pupils caught them shouting at one another by the midden. Another time they quarrelled over the pitchforks; and often David would have hit Pat if she hadn't been a girl.

He became bad-tempered at home too, until one day his mother cornered him and said, "Oh, David, what's the matter? Something's troubling you."

But he wouldn't say, because, in spite of everything, he and Pat were still in partnership and he was determined to behave as though everything was as it had always been.

On this occasion he turned to his mother and said, "There's nothing the matter. Why do you think there is?"

"Well, you're gloomy enough. You're not yourself. Anyone can see that," she answered.

"I expect it's the remains of the 'flu," he replied, avoiding his mother's eyes.

If it hadn't been for Tornado's progress, he would have been really sick at heart at this time. But she was improving by leaps and bounds, and now March had come the ground was drier and he could school her more. She was beginning to feel relaxed and supple, her collected paces had improved, her neck had gained muscle; sometimes when David stood back and looked at her gazing over her box door, he'd feel a lump in his throat because she looked so lovely, and for a moment everything else would be forgotten.

The first one-day event was fifty miles away – at the end of April. By that time he would be old enough to compete.

He wrote for the schedule, and when it came showed it to Pat.

"I think Tornado will have to go in the Novice Class, don't you?" he asked.

89

"Yes. Seems the best idea," she replied.

"What shall I enter her as – property of the Elm Tree Riding School?"

"Better under your own name, I should think," Pat replied.

"But she belongs to both of us," said David.

"They may not like riding schools competing. For goodness' sake, let's enter her under your name," Pat replied.

There didn't seem any point in arguing. David filled up the entry form.

"Are you sure you don't mind me entering?" he asked.

"Why on earth should I?" replied Pat.

After that everything seemed settled, and there was only a month left, which didn't seem any time at all to David.

His mother was pleased to hear that he was entering. His father said, "Remember to wear your hat. There's a good few crashes from time to time."

"Do you think your horse can do it?" asked his mother.

"Yes. Easily," replied David.

He worried most about Tornado's show jumping. She was very erratic; across country she took more trouble, she was bold when it came to timber and jumped with plenty of scope. But there didn't seem enough time to improve her any more, and he remembered from past experience that there never does seem enough time – in the end one just hopes for the best.

So he didn't worry, and at last April came, and the fields were suddenly green and birds started to build nests, and Pat spent three days in London with her mother buying clothes, and the Easter holidays began.

The Rodeo Display

Before the one-day event there was a show. Pat and David entered John and Folly in the juvenile jumping and Julia, who had improved, on Swallow. After some discussion, they also entered David and Tornado for the Best Riding Horse Class, and the Foxhunter Jumping Competition.

They entered various pupils for the gymkhana events. Pat and David decided to ride Swallow and Folly in the Open Musical Chairs, and the Handy Hunter.

It was a small show and was holding a Foxhunter Jumping Competition for the first time.

The Riding Horse Class usually contained a variety of horses.

"It'll be useful experience for Tornado," David said as they made out the entries, which must catch the next post if they were to be in time.

"Yes; and fun for all of us too. It seems years since I've ridden in a show," Pat replied.

They had repainted their jumps, which looked professional now. David had made many of them himself, including the cavaletti, which weren't quite straight.

Pat seemed anxious that they should all do well at the show, and David's hopes rose a little. Folly and Tornado seemed at the top of their form. The smaller ponies were good at bending, at apple and bucket and musical chairs.

On the morning of the show everyone's hopes were high. David and Pat rose at four-thirty, because they wanted to plait all the ponies' manes, because there was Mistletoe and a lot of Suzy to wash, because there was a seven-mile hack over, and the first class was at ten o'clock.

It was one of those wild April mornings when the clouds seem to be chasing each other in the sky, when anything could happen – sun or showers, wind or rain, or maybe in the end a cloudless day.

David could only think, 'One more week, and then I shall be riding Tornado across country.' It mattered more than anything; during April it was all he lived for.

They started with the washing, Pat on Mistletoe, David on Suzy. At first it was dark and they worked by electric light, but presently dawn came, and later the pupils who had offered to help.

At eight o'clock Pat and David had a hasty breakfast in

the Lewishams' kitchen. Afterwards they started to plait, standing on buckets with needles stuck in their jerseys, reels of thread and scissors in their pockets or lodged on their horses' necks, parting manes, counting, 'One, two, three, four, five, six, seven plaits and a forelock,' cursing softly when their horses moved.

Julia plaited Sinbad. His mane was bristly, and when she had finished his plaits stood on end, but there wasn't time to do them again.

By nine o'clock the clouds had gone. The sun was shining. It seemed a perfect day.

David and Pat were behind the schedule they had worked out laboriously the day before. Tempers were short. John, Julia, Caroline and Peter took refuge in the saddle-room. Pat snapped at David; David snapped back.

But at last they were ready, all riding out of the yard together towards the sun, and David was laughing, saying, "Only five minutes behind schedule after all."

And Pat was saying, "Swallow's awfully fresh."

And all of them were imagining the events they were entered for, hoping there wouldn't be too many entries, that the bending posts would be the right distance apart, the jumps solid and well spaced.

And now suddenly there was magic in the morning which spoke of summer, of long sunlit days, of light nights and early dawns.

'I feel happy,' thought David, 'so happy. If only I could grasp these moments in my hand and hold them for ever!'

And Pat felt at peace. She didn't long for anything else; she was content to be riding along the sunlit road to the show.

John was nervous and happy at the same time. To be jumping Folly was an enormous responsibility; it would be so easy to let her down. If she didn't jump a clear round, it would be his fault. But he was happy, too, because out of all the children at the riding school he had been chosen to ride her.

Caroline was thinking, 'I bet I knock down a bending

pole.' Peter was far away, wondering how it felt to ride on sand. Julia was thinking, 'I must try to sit still. I hope the course isn't big,' seeing jumps following each other, painted poles, black brushes, glaring walls, stark white gates.

Soon they came to notices, *To the Show*, and Pat looked at her watch and said, "We've plenty of time."

The ponies were still fresh, and Tornado seemed to sense excitement in the air and started to jog. Presently a horse-box passed them, followed by a cattle-truck, and they could see a string of ponies ahead, and in the distance flags and tents.

And David thought, 'This is what we've worked for during the last year, to be riding to a show with our ponies ridden by pupils, to have someone to jump Folly and Swallow, to have a mare of our own like Tornado.'

And he felt a rush of pride as they came to the show ground, and as they turned in he looked back at the ponies and thought how nice they looked – Mistletoe a sparkling grey, her neat head accentuated by plaits, Sinbad a shining black with gleaming tack, Suzy gay with her tail high, her four legs a spotless white, Swallow and Folly fit and shining with breeding in their carriage, muscles in the right places, round, well-shod hoofs. And they're all ours, he thought, and somewhere a band was striking up and everything brought back memories – the horse-boxes parked in rows, ponies tied to railings, people in jodhs and dungarees clutching dandy brushes. 'This is my life,' he thought. 'To me it means as much as the grease-paint and the stage to the actor,' and his heart was singing as they trotted on across the field with the band playing and the sun shining.

Later Caroline and Peter rode Mistletoe and Sinbad in the Pony Class, while David and Pat and the children's parents watched from the ring ropes.

They both let their ponies bunch, and whenever a steward spoke to Peter he called out "What?" in a loud voice which everyone could hear.

Finally, Caroline and Mistletoe were awarded third prize and Peter left the ring with the rest of the back row.

After that John and Julia rode in the Larger Pony Class, and Swallow was awarded second prize, and Folly shied and John, who was thinking about removing his hat if he was handed a rosette, fell off. He was very apologetic when he came out with the tail end of the front row.

"Gosh! I'm sorry," he said. "I couldn't have been much worse, could I?"

"It happens to everyone at times," replied David.

"We didn't expect her to win, anyway," said Pat.

They all had lunch together, sitting under a big chestnut tree, while their mounts munched oats and bran and more horse-boxes arrived.

Everything was new to Tornado; she looked at it with wild eyes, and dug up the ground with all four feet.

David tried to calm her.

"She's getting absolutely filthy," Pat said.

"She'll be tired before she begins to jump," exclaimed Julia.

David led Tornado round the show ground, and gradually she grew calmer. He kept meeting people who said, "Hullo, David. What's that you've got?" – people he hadn't seen for ages.

"It's Tornado. I'm jumping her," he would reply.

And they would say, "Is she any good?" or "Where did she come from?"

And they treated everything he said seriously because he had done so well as a juvenile two years before.

Their seriousness frightened him, so that presently he found himself saying, "I'm jumping her, but she isn't much good. We'll probably smash up the course."

But they only replied "Oh, ah . . ." or "Do you think so?" or simply "Go on."

He returned to the chestnut tree to find Pat putting John and Julia up.

"We need a practice jump," she said.

He tied up Tornado and left her pawing the ground. He

had a funny feeling now in the pit of his stomach. People seemed to know where Tornado had come from. Today was her big moment. "Supposing she won't go into the ring? Or shies at the jumps? Or refuses three times?' he thought, pulling a pole out of a hedge, calling to Pat, "Will you hold the other end?"

Swallow refused the pole; Folly jumped, taking off miles in front, landing way out on the other side.

The competitors for Class Four, Juvenile Jumping, were being called into the collecting ring. Swallow cleared the pole, then the ponies each jumped a second time before David went away to get Tornado ready for the Riding Horse Class, which came after the Juvenile Jumping.

His parents had come, and Susan with a young man on a motor-bike.

"Well, best of luck," his mother said.

"Rather ride a motor-bike any day," muttered the young man.

"Go on with you," said Susan.

Tornado was fresh and silly. Her back was up when he mounted and started to ride her outside the ring. Swallow and Folly hadn't jumped yet. He could see Pat waiting with John and Julia. A clear round was announced. The course was small and there was nothing particularly difficult about it.

'It ought to be nothing to Folly,' thought David and was sorry for John competing for the first time on a well-known juvenile jumper. He remembered jumping Folly the year before last, when he was younger and lighter. She had been at the top of her form then and always jumped clear the first time round. She was wonderful to ride, he remembered, and the less practice she had between shows the better. And now she was jumping, he saw, suddenly glancing at the ring, effortlessly in her old style, clearing each jump as though it hardly existed, with that calm look in her eye which had come with experience.

His heart lifted a little as she cleared the last fence. Without thinking, he had jumped with John, felt Folly's stride lengthen at each fence, felt the sudden relief when it was over and they were cantering out of the ring.

He cantered across the show ground to congratulate John.

"It was Folly," John said, giving the brown pony oats from his pocket.

"Ssh. Swallow's in the ring," said Pat.

Julia was suffering from an acute attack of nerves. They could all see that, and David felt sorry for her. She seemed to lose the use of her seat and legs as she rode Swallow towards the first jump and Pat started jumping about and crying, "Legs, legs," as though Julia could hear her all across the ring. Swallow refused. Pat groaned. David said, "Don't let Folly look."

After that Julia seemed to pull herself together and rode quite a creditable round.

"Three faults," said Pat as she came out. Julia was apologetic, but they all said it didn't matter, and David said, "Jolly good for your first time."

Later there was a jump-off and John lost his balance over the gate, which Folly hit, which meant four faults. Finally, she was third, and David said, "Jolly good. Another rosette," and rode away on Tornado and tried to get her going properly before he was called into the ring.

When the moment came she went better than he had dared to hope; it was as though she knew this was a test for her. Though she led off on the wrong leg once, and shied at the jumps the first time round, she was full of impulsion, and under perfect control. David could feel the judges looking at Tornado. There were a great many better-looking horses in the class, but manners counted, and hers were good enough to counteract her goose-rump.

They were called into fourth place, and now the judges started to ride the horses. David dismounted, tightened his girths, and let down his stirrups. Pat came in with a rubber and polished Tornado.

"She's going awfully well," she said.

There were two judges, a tall slim man in Newmarket boots, breeches, checked jacket, bowler hat and a quiet tie, and a farmer, ruddy-featured, heavily built, who rode more by determination than anything else.

It was the second one who came across and said, "Can I ride your mare?"

David held the stirrup while he mounted with a heave and a grunt.

"She's bigger than she looks," the judge said.

He could feel Tornado quivering all over as the judge picked up the reins. Her tail was between her legs, her ears back. David wanted to say, "Ride her carefully. Don't rush her." But the judge wasn't a pupil, and he most likely knew much more about horses than David.

The other judge was mounting a grey further down the row. The band was playing. The ring was totally surrounded by cars.

The farmer clapped his heels against Tornado and she rushed forward with a jump. Her back was up, her ears more back than forward. David thought, 'Thank goodness I pulled up the girths,' and then Tornado started to buck in earnest and his heart seemed to stand still. She gave great twists to her body as she bucked – it was like a rodeo display. And suddenly the crowd was silent, and all eyes were on the ring. David could feel this awful silence and prayed, "Don't let him fall off." But now the farmer had lost a stirrup, and David rushed forward and tried to catch hold of Tornado and the crowd started to talk again, and the mare went on bucking. And although it seemed eternity to David, actually it was all over in a matter of seconds – the farmer judge was on the ground and Tornado, bucking still, was careering out of the ring. The competitors were all talking now, and everyone was rushing towards the judge on the ground, who was trying to get up, and groaning. David thought, 'Pat will catch Tornado. She always said she was a one-man mare, and she was right. We'll never sell her.'

The judge stood up and wiped his face with a handker-chief. David waited to see what he would say. All the competitors stopped talking.

"Hadn't you better go after your mare?" the judge asked

It was like a rodeo display